The Grove

The Grove

by Ken Zahn

Southern Lion Books

First Printing

Published by
Southern Lion Books
1280 Westminster Way
Madison, Georgia 30650

southernlionbooks.com

Manufactured in the United States of America.

Library of Congress Control No. 2008938117

ISBN: 978-0-9794203-7-5

The paper in this book meets the guidelines for permanence
and durability of the Committee on Production Guidelines
for Book Longevity of the Council on Library Resources.

Chapter illustrations by Mary-Frances Burt

Dedicated to my wife Kathy and my daughter Audrey

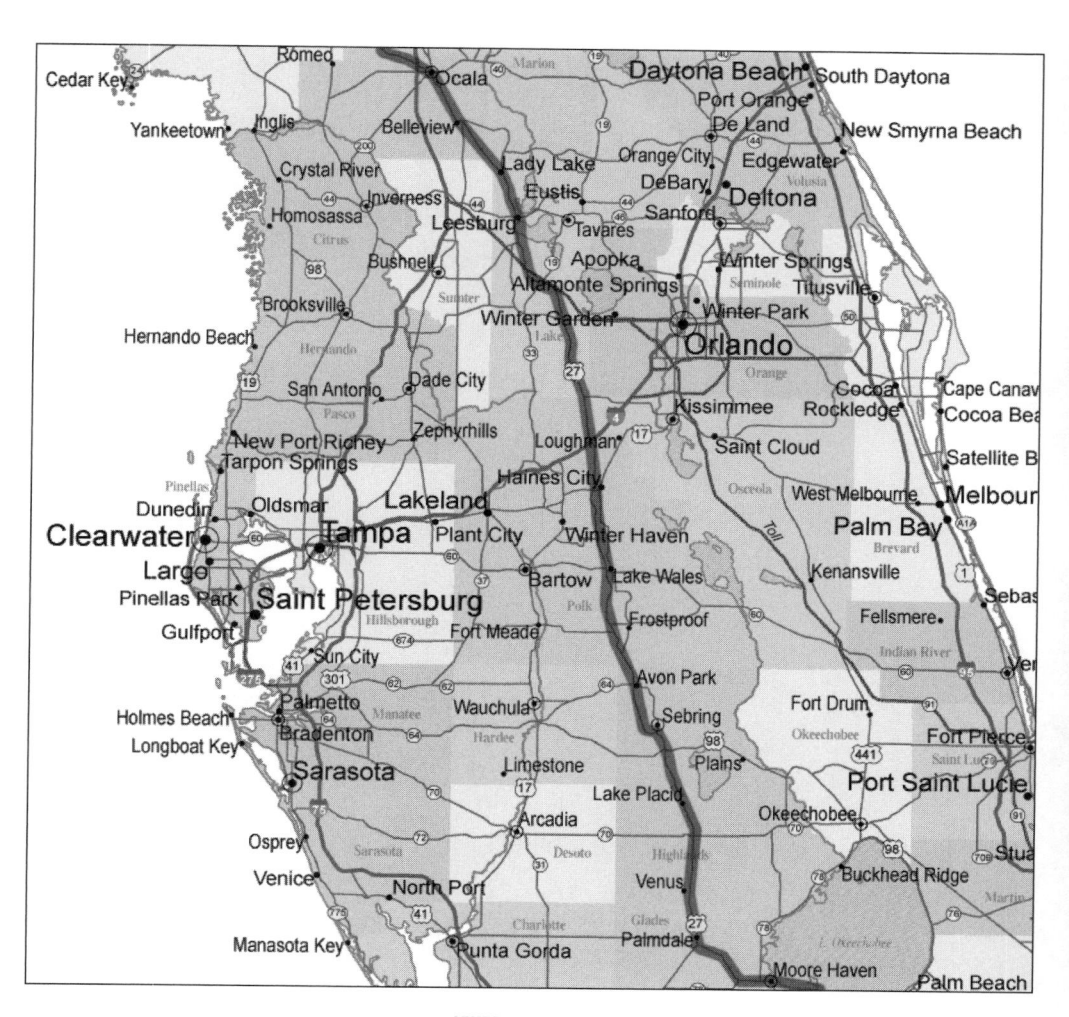

CENTRAL FLORIDA

CHAPTER ONE

Arthur

"No! I won't do this. I won't travel across the state to handle another hopeless financial planning client."

This was the start of a telephone call I received from Harry, a good client and friend. Harry was responsible for referring many wealthy clients to me in my early years of practice. He was the main reason I could semi-retire in my early sixties. Harry was not about to give up.

"Arthur, you owe me big time."

I groaned inwardly.

"No, I already paid you back by helping your less wealthy friends out of financial trouble. Those clients couldn't even afford to pay me, so I didn't even charge a fee." I, too, was determined to "win" this conversation.

Relentlessly, Harry continued.

"Arthur, this is just the kind of case you love—an old land-poor Florida cracker case with no possible solution. Other reputable financial planners have tried to work with this lady but have either been run off or have given up."

Only Harry would use the term "cracker." Years ago, Florida cowboys used whips to move the cattle. Hence the term cracker stuck to multi-generation Floridians.

I considered feigning a disconnected telephone line, but decided otherwise.

"Listen Harry, if you think that giving an old dog a good bone to chew on will change this dog's mind, forget it. After thirty years of practice, I've had my fill of incurable client situations."

I prayed that my argument was good enough to get me out of this.

"Arthur, I know you don't need the money. We all know your existing practice provides more than enough spending money, but this client is willing to compensate you in ways other than monetary. She has a collection of old Lionel trains that she inherited from her father. Some of the trains are in their original boxes in mint condition. If you can solve her problem, she is willing to sell them to you dirt cheap."

Now Harry had my attention. He knows that I'm passionate about my train collection. I felt myself being sucked in.

"How old are the trains?" I asked.

"I think some date back to 1915, and some could be even older."

Two things will tempt me—old cars and old trains. Antique cars are beyond my financial means, but old trains are relatively inexpensive and fun. My collection is still small. Harry knew I was looking for unique trains. And, in mint condition!

"Ok, Harry, you have my attention. Who is this client?" God, I hated losing this tug-of war to Harry, but old trains are just too tempting to ignore.

"The client's name is Alexandria Thompson-Gibbons. She goes by Alex and is sixty-seven years old. She is fourth-generation Floridian. Her great-grandfather came to Florida originally to raise cattle. The cattle business was so successful that he bought up all the surrounding land. Around 1900 her grandfather started a small orange grove on part of the land-holdings to stabilize his income. Seems like he'd become too dependent on beef prices. Then, Alex's father converted the grazing land to orange groves and expanded the land-holdings. When you meet Alex, you'll find out that she's had financial problems over the last few years. Plus, she's had some health problems as well. She needs your help, Arthur."

"What kind of health problems?" My interest was piqued. Damn Harry!

"High blood pressure. Alex is lean and mean. She has a reputation for being ornery and losing her temper easily. One financial planner made the mistake of suggesting she sell the grove. She ran him off with a sawed-off shotgun. As you know, hypertension and temper are a lethal combination."

I sat bolt upright. "Holy crap, Harry! You know I hate guns." Was he out of his mind? Surely, Harry didn't expect me to risk my life doing something I didn't want to do in the first place.

"Alex is a crack shot. She wouldn't kill you." Harry chuckled. I'm glad he was amused because I wasn't.

"Ok, bottom line. Don't lie to me. What happened to the financial planner?"

"Nothing," said Harry. "The sight of the shotgun was enough to make him wet his pants. But she did make a slight alteration to the car of a land developer who also made the same suggestion."

"What does 'slight alteration' mean?" This was getting worse by the minute. Harry should have told me this first.

"She shot out the tail lights of his Mercedes with her handgun."

"This story is unbelievable!" I said. "I can't wait to meet this spitfire. Is she in jail?"

"No, seems she's had a romantic relationship with the Sheriff since her husband died. The Sheriff had the tail lights replaced and assured the land developer he would look the other way if the developer ever needed him to."

"Wow! This is like something out of an old 1960s novel about Florida. And you want me to jump into this cesspool?" I was beginning to doubt whether Harry really valued my friendship or my life!

"Yep, as fast as you can. It'll only take a day or two to figure this puzzle out. I told Alex you would be coming and to get the trains out. There no hotel within miles. So, she'll have the guest room ready for you."

"This is a setup, Harry, and you know it! Ok, I'll do this, but we're even now. I will have paid *all* my debts to you."

"Call me when you get back, Arthur."

"Sure. If you don't hear from me, take care of my funeral arrangements."

When he laughed, it sent a shiver through me.

4

CHAPTER TWO

Alex

I have lived in Tampa for nearly forty years. I love Old Florida, but I'm not so sure I like the new one. Growth along the I-4 corridor from Tampa to Orlando has been phenomenal. The state of Florida took over thirty years to wake up and improve the road. This morning I headed east toward Orlando and, then, south on US-27 west of Orlando. Some of the highest land in the southern part of the state is along US-27. It has a gentle roll, and Alex's acreage was along this spine of land. Alex was expecting my arrival late morning. I had suggested to her that we enjoy an early lunch before getting down to business.

I was anxious to meet this woman. Alex lived beyond all the sprawling development and congestion. The nearest so-called town was small, about one mile square, and reasonably old for Florida. Old US-27 used to run through it, but now the divided highway was to the west. As a result, the town's growth had stood still. Due to a lack of tourist attractions and local businesses, there were no motels or hotels newer than 1950. I was glad Harry had made arrangements for me to stay with Alex. He mentioned that her house was historic. I had never heard of a historic Florida home that was actually some-

5

one's residence; at least not the way Harry used the term "historic."

He said there was no sign on US-27 that marked the narrow unpaved road leading to Alex's home. He gave me the exact mileage from I-4 to the turn. I made sure to set my odometer to zero after leaving the interstate. As much as I hate to admit it, I was feeling a sense of anticipation—a welcome relief from my original dread.

Each step towards her house was like a step backwards in time. First I traveled the now speedy I-4, then the congested US-27, and last a dirt road through the grove to a house built around the turn of the century. I was about to discover what Harry meant by historic. The house was stately and well-maintained with a wrap-around porch. Sitting among the trees on a rise (a hill to most Floridians!), the house was two stories high. One thing was immediately noticeable; the windows were all open in spite of the fact that it was late summer. Yipes! Fortunately, I'm cold-blooded and a casual dresser. Now I knew what Harry meant by historic.

A woman with golden hair answered my knock and opened the screen door to the inviting porch. She introduced herself as Goldie and explained that she was the housekeeper/cook. As she extended her hand in welcome, I introduced myself to her.

She said she recognized me from Harry's description. I hoped she didn't notice my confused look. How would someone describe me to a stranger? Goldie escorted me into the living room.

"Alex will be downstairs shortly," she said, "and lunch will be served on the side veranda."

I glanced around and saw a room that was simple, comfortable, and extremely neat. There was nothing pretentious here. Everything had both a purpose and a place. I took a few minutes to freshen up in the nearby washroom while awaiting

Alex's entrance. Luckily, a late morning breeze was beginning to stir.

Upon meeting Alex, I realized she and I were alike. She was a no-nonsense, get-to-the-point conversationalist. So am I. Ignoring pleasantries and small talk, she cut to the chase.

"Harry says you're ok. That you take on hopeless clients. That you keep an open mind."

Was she insulting me? Not all of my clients are hopeless. I decided not to allow her negative attitude to deter me.

"I was hoping to take advantage of our informal lunch to gather some general information before we get into details. Tell me about yourself and the grove."

While Goldie served us lunch, Alex told me about herself. As she talked, I studied her closely. She was slender, and she had an ageless attractiveness about her. At age sixty-seven, she appeared to be the perfect matriarch. "The Grove" was her home and her life. As an only child, she was raised like a son. She had been taught to hunt with the best of men. Her real love was the land and the trees. As a result, she went to the university as an "ag" student. She was more knowledgeable about agriculture than her bookish professors. Arthur could tell that Alex had been a striking beauty, and he imagined that although the sorority girls were taken aback by the fact that she would return after class at the end of the day with horse-shit on her boots, beauty and old cracker money had won out.

She met Tom Gibbons when they were both sophomores. Tom played fullback on the football team. He was a respected player but not a star on the team. He was easygoing and fun, qualities Alex knew she lacked. She realized she had found her match. Her pursuit of him was subtle but unrelenting. After a year of dating, he proposed, and they decided to marry after graduation. After graduation and marriage, Alex and Tom lived near the Grove. Alex helped her father run the Grove while Tom taught at the local high school. Life was simple, and Alex and Tom liked it that way.

Almost four years after her marriage, Alex's parents were killed in an auto accident. Although grieving the death of her parents, Alex's pragmatic side took over. She realized that the IRS valued the Grove at $10 million and that there were no liquid assets with which to pay estate taxes. Unfortunately, her parents had not planned for an untimely joint death. After a bitter IRS battle, the value of the Grove (the economic value of the land) was reduced to $8 million. Between taking out loans on the land and convincing the IRS to let her pay the taxes over a period of years rather than as a lump sum, Alex inherited the entire property. She gifted half of the property to Tom after the 1981 Tax Act allowed spousal gifts without limits.[1]

Life became tough. The estate taxes due at Alex's parents' deaths really strapped Alex and Tom for cash, but they managed to pay off the taxes and to improve the Grove. Tom learned to love the Grove, especially when the orange trees bloomed. The marriage produced three children. Twelve years ago, Tom died of a heart attack, which was quite a shock to Alex. After that, she had to rely on herself. Alex never involved her children, now adults, in the ownership of the Grove. She just didn't trust them with the property. I noticed that she had become strangely unemotional, almost removed, when speaking about the children. Since Tom's death, Alex has had the Grove and two grandchildren to keep her satisfied. After lunch we got down to basics.

"Let's get to the bottom line. What happens if you die?"

Alex's response was immediate and forthright. "The IRS will be like bears to honey. One land developer offered me $100 million for the land. My CPA and attorney don't know what to do. As long as I'm living, I don't want to sell the land. My dad would roll over in his grave."

[1] See Glossary, 1, 12, and 20.

"What about your children?" I asked.

Again Alex's response lacked hesitation. "Worthless as tits on a boar. Wait until you meet them. I told them you were the best financial planner in the U.S. They're scared that either I will outlive them or that you will have some complicated or sophisticated plan that will deprive them of their inheritance. Are you really that good?"

Now it was my turn to answer with certainty. "No."

Alex frowned. "All right, you're not the best. At least you're truthful... and you're all I've got. What are you going to do next?"

"Ask you some more questions. Harry said that you're a top-notch land manager but that the financial affairs of the Grove are handled by your CPA. Before I meet with him today, what do you call the Grove? Does it have a name?"

"No, my grandfather hated self-important people who named land after themselves. We've always just called it the Grove. The land, the house, the business—everything. It's 'The Grove.' However, after I gifted the land to Tom, we formed an S corporation. The name is AT-TG, Inc. Tom and I just used our initials. But I'd rather you refer to it as 'The Grove.' "

I closed my notebook and put my pen behind my ear. I needed some time alone to think.

"Ok, I'll see you later. Be ready for more questions. I would like to get as much data today as possible so I can sleep on it. Financial planning needs some fermenting."

A true financial plan is developed after a financial planner has collected all the data. At this point I had no idea how to solve this puzzle. Hopefully the meeting with the CPA would give me a starting place.

S corporations have been around for over fifty years.[2] One of the problems with regular corporations is the so-called "double taxation." If a regular corporation retains income at

[2] *See Glossary 6b*

year-end, it is taxed once at the corporate level. Then when the earnings are distributed to the shareholders, the shareholders are taxed a second time on the dividends they receive. The S corporation status eliminated the double taxation. The corporation's income or losses pass through to the shareholders and are reported on the shareholders' personal tax return.

Personally, I like operating as a regular corporation, especially after the passage of the 2003 Tax Act.[3] Dividend distributions are now at a maximum 15% tax rate. Regular corporations allow for more employee benefits for employee shareholders. The conversation with her CPA should prove interesting. At least I could work with the concept of stocks. Corporations, whether regular or S-type, present more planning opportunities. If she filed as a sole proprietor, I probably would be limited in possible financial planning solutions. I planned to review at least two to three years of S corporate 1120S returns and her personal 1040 returns with her CPA. I hoped he had plenty of time. Glancing at my watch, I saw that I had a few minutes to get myself organized before leaving to see Alex's CPA. As I climbed the stairs to my room, the air got hotter with each step. The afternoon heat was setting in; I hoped the CPA's office wasn't also "historic."

[3] See Glossary, 6a.

CHAPTER THREE

Jack Holden

Alex's original CPA died some years ago. His son, Jack Holden, now represented her. John "Jack" Holden had a typical one-person office in a small town. As I parked, I thought to myself that Orlando and the big guy national firms hadn't caught up with him yet. I wasn't sure if that was a good thing or not. As I pushed open the heavy wood door to his office, I was met by a blast of cold air. No need to worry about the Florida heat in here. Jack slammed a file drawer shut and spun around. He didn't look pleased. I put on my friendliest smile as I shook hands with Jack and introduced myself.

"Hi, Jack, I'm Arthur. I assume that Alex told you to expect me."

Jack did not attempt to disguise his annoyance and displeasure. "Yes, I thought she had her fill of so-called financial planners. You guys think you're smart, but you don't know the difference between a 1065 and an 1120."

My dislike of Jack was immediate. My smile disappeared. This self-righteous jerk was going to be a pain in my ass.

"Listen, Jack, don't get huffy with me. I came here with an open mind to get facts, not grief. By the way, I've been incorporated since 1981 and file my own corporate 1120. So, let's get on with the S corporation 1120S information."

Jack hesitated and shifted his eyes downward. He thought I was wasting his time. I gathered he did not think much of financial planners.

"Ok, what do you want to know?"

"Well, before we start, can you give me some background on the corporation?"

Jack waved me to a chair across from his desk. I sat down.

"As you may or may not know, my father handled the Grove's financial affairs with Alex's father and then with Alex after her father died. I took over when my father died. Actually, the Grove did very well until 2004. It escaped the terrible freezes of the 1980s. Are you from this area? Remember the three hurricanes that blew through this area in 2004? The orange trees were stripped but survived. Then, in 2005 another hurricane slightly affected the trees. As a result, cash flow over those years was nonexistent. Alex had to bankroll the cash flow from her personal money."

Jack paused, and I took advantage of the opportunity to ask another question. "Do you handle Alex's personal financial affairs?"

"Yes and no," he answered. "I file her personal 1040, but it's very simple because most of her expenses are on the corporation's 1120S. The Grove owns the house she lives in."

"How badly did 2004 and 2005 affect her?" I asked.

"Well, it stripped her of a lot of personal cash and created carry forward corporate losses that she is still using up. So, her personal cash position is improving dramatically because her income is mostly tax-free because of the losses."

I decided to shift my line of questioning away from taxes and asked, "Didn't she have crop insurance?"

Jack didn't appear defensive. Apparently insurance wasn't an issue with him. "No, the winter freezes don't usually come this far south, and hurricanes normally lose their punch this far inland. She felt safe without crop insurance. Plus, she's a wealthy woman who lives frugally."

"Jack, since I'm a Johnny-come-lately and don't know the family like you do, do you have any suggestions on what Alex should do?"

"No." Jack's quick admittance seemed sincere.

"What about her children?"

"Well, when the corporate cash flow died after 2004 and Alex had to fund the operating expenses, she cut off her children's salaries. The kids are still pissed."

Hmmmm. The kids were on the payroll. That was news to me. Alex hadn't told me that. I thought they weren't involved. At the risk of sounding assuming, I offered my opinion.

"I have this gut feeling they don't do any work at the Grove," I commented.

"You're right, but they are on the books as employees and get W-2s, company cars, and various benefits."

I knew my work was cut out for me. I had too many unanswered questions and suspicions. Too bad I only had a day or two to find a solution to this nightmare.

"I hope you have some time this afternoon because we're going to go line by line through the last five years of corporate tax returns. Alex is paying us both by the hour. Let's work together and try to give her her money's worth."

Jack and I spent the next few hours perusing tax returns and various other documents. Looking back beyond 2004, I discovered that the Grove had made a lot of excess profits.

"Jack, why didn't you convert the S corporation to a regular C corporation?"

"I don't believe in regular corporations," Jack said caustically.

"Any reason why not?"

"No."

But I knew. Year-end planning with S corporations is simple. The income and losses just pass to the shareholders. With a regular C corporation, the CPA really needs to do some bookkeeping with the client before year-end. A regular C puts a lot of year-end planning stress on the CPA. No one likes to work extra hours during the Christmas season. Because I am not a CPA or a tax attorney, I just moved on with my questions. It really didn't matter whether Alex had an S corporation or regular corporation. I could always switch an S to a regular corporation if that's the way the planning turned out.

I knew what I was in for with the returns—buried expenses that weren't legitimate. With Alex's potential net worth, the IRS would take a close look at these business statements if she died. In addition, I needed to know the real value of the business after I cut all the fat out.

"I see that prior to 2004 the officers' salaries were substantial. Who are the officers of the company?"

Jack switched his reading glasses from the end of his nose to the top of his head and stretched back in his chair.

"Well, Alex owns all the stock and is the president, and her three children are officers."

"I didn't think the children were involved in the company's operations," I questioned.

"They're not involved, Arthur. They just get paid."

My confusion must have shown. Jack reiterated his abhorrence for Alex's children.

"Listen Arthur, these three leeches are tenacious. I call them the 3-Ds: dull, drunk, and drugged. If Alex didn't pay them, she would have to gift them the money. This way Uncle Sam is subsidizing them."

"I see the salaries almost zeroed out in 2005 and 2006 after the hurricanes in 2004 and 2005."

"Arthur, if you remember, I previously told you that when Alex had to finance the corporation's deficiencies, she cut off all salaries. The 3Ds went berserk. Salaries have picked up some, but the bitching is continuous. Since I write the checks, I get the calls."

I had moved my chair next to Jack's so I could see the 1120S. I was going line by line with him. Soon another item caught my eye.

"The only vehicle I saw at the Grove was a ten-year-old pickup truck. What's with the company cars item? It looks substantial." I asked the question even though I was pretty sure I already knew the answer.

"The company buys cars for the 3Ds and pays for gas and upkeep. The cars are expensive."

I was shocked at Jack's lack of concern.

"Jack, this is totally illegal. There is absolutely no business use. Are the children charged with any of the costs?" I asked incredulously.

"No, that's one nice thing about an 1120S corporate filing; you can bury all kinds of expenses."

I wondered why I didn't just hang up on Harry when he called. Why do I punish myself with other's incompetence and dishonesty? I don't need this headache.

"Is there any substantiation provided?" I asked.

"No."

"Jack, I wouldn't be proud of this. I hate to look at some of these other items. Is this the tip of the iceberg?"

"Yes."

"Ok, let's move on. Travel expenses? I got the impression that Alex didn't go anywhere."

"She doesn't. The kids are doing the traveling. I call this business meetings and conventions."

"You have got to be kidding. I suppose the trips are to Las Vegas, Reno, and maybe Mexico."

"You've got it," Jack smirked.

"Where is the 50% meal allowance?"

"Also buried. Listen, this is a multi-million dollar corporation that is usually very profitable. The IRS just looks at the bottom line so far because she pays taxes...plenty of taxes. The Grove has always spilled a lot of taxable income into Alex's 1040 return. There has never been an audit." Jack sounded almost proud. His true colors were really showing now.

Even though I was disgusted at this point, my face showed nothing. I had to get through the 1120S. That was my purpose in coming.

"This next item is a bit much. Where is the boat, and what is it used for?"

"It's on the lake at the Grove. The Grove's water supply comes from the lake. Alex doesn't have any un-depreciated equipment anymore; all work on the Grove is outsourced. So I listed it as equipment, and I've been depreciating it."

"I suppose that it's a ski boat and you expensed it under 179?"[4]

"Yes, some of it. The rest is being depreciated."

"I suppose you also are burying some country club dues?" I was astonished.

"You got it."

Unbelievable! I couldn't hide my irritation any longer. Did this guy have any scruples? I got up from my chair and started pacing around the office. I could see this was upsetting Jack, but I had had enough.

"Jack, I came here to solve Alex's potential estate tax problem. One of my many contacts is a publicly traded company that might be interested in doing a stock swap. These financials aren't going to fly with the public company's CPAs. They're

[4] See Glossary, 17.

going to eat you alive. Your creative accounting will have to be amended," I lectured.

Jack swung his chair around to face me. "What! Alex wouldn't sell out. She loves the Grove." The smirk of self-assurance on Jack's face made me more determined to press on.

"I'm going to talk to her about it as soon as possible. This whole thing is making me sick, but let's continue. The next area is medical expenses. These numbers are unbelievable."

"The company provides group medical insurance for Alex's three children and her daughter Cindy's two children. It's a good plan," Jack said, trying to reassure me.

"Jack, I know medical insurance premiums, and these numbers are way beyond anything I can calculate, given the children and grandchildren's ages."

"Well, the corporation has a medical reimbursement plan for all medical claims not covered by the health plan for the employees. Alex has Medicare and a Medicare supplemental plan she pays for personally," Jack explained.

"Ok, the children are fairly young. These extra company-paid expenses shouldn't be that exceptional. Dental work and eyeglasses or eye exams are minor expenses. So do I have to dig through your files, or are you going to tell me the bad news?"

"You big city smart-asses just don't know how things work in small towns."

My prying had become less of an inconvenience for Jack and more of a threat. I didn't even attempt to conceal my indignation.

"What do you mean by that? Illegal financial dealings aren't limited to small companies or small towns. The big-city boys are just more earnest about it. The financial press I read is full of illegal financial dealings. I've got a feeling there is even more dirt. Let's get this over with."

I could see I'd have to fight item by item. Judging by the dollar amount shown, I knew the next area was full of illegal activity. "Jack," I asked, "What's with the medical expenses?"

"The medical areas include all of Cindy's cosmetic surgery. She had two sets of breast augmentation plus a series of nip and tuck operations. Yes, I know, all nondeductible expenses. The problem is that, with Cindy, one surgery always leads to another. A few years ago, she was in the middle of a few procedures when Alex stopped authorizing any money. Cindy went ballistic."

I shouldn't have been surprised, but I was. This family was really abusing the "reimbursement for medical claims not covered" thing under medical reimbursement.

Jack continued. "Then, there's Dawn, the druggie. When Dawn hits rock bottom, Alex has to send her to a rehab center. Luckily, the Sheriff is aware of Dawn's addiction. One night she almost killed a kid with her car. With a little hush money, the Sheriff made the kid's family happy and the police file disappeared."

Good God! Hush money!

"Ok, I'll let you off with where the hush money comes from, but this is incredible. How long has this been going on, and how much does it amount to per year? I need a number to work with. It'll take forever and a day to figure out the real earnings of the Grove."

"Well, between the wages, business expenses, medical, and other items, it ranges between $500,000 and $1 million per year except for years 2005 and 2006. It's still on the low side now since 2006. Alex nearly bust a gut putting up the money to fund the bad years."

"This has to stop! Alex must put an end to all of this, and this is a good time while it's still on the low side. If the IRS shows up on your doorstep, they are going to nail you for aiding and abetting and Alex for millions in taxes and penalties. And it won't be hard to prove. Do you handle your other clients this way?"

"No. But let me finish telling you about Alex's children. Wait until you meet Gibby, her son. He is some kind of mean-tempered son-of-a-bitch. One day he showed up here with a gun, and when I balked on giving him money for a Las Vegas trip, he shot a hole in the wall there behind the picture. I didn't report the incident for fear of being beaten up or killed. I know that's a poor excuse, but it is the truth. I assure you my other clients are handled properly."

To my surprise, I found myself feeling a little sorry for Jack. Alex had dumped her worthless kids in Jack's lap and expected him to take care of their financial whims. It sounded like they harassed Jack to get what they wanted.

"Ok, Jack, but let me leave you with my comments about S corporations versus regular corporations. S corporations can't do net operating loss carry backs (NOLs).[5] The losses in 2005 and 2006 could have been carried back to those good years of 2003 and 2004. With a regular corporation, you could have taken the losses on an amended return. The tax refund money received from 2003 and 2004 would have subsidized her cash flow during those lean years. In addition, I feel that S corporation employee shareholders are treated shabbily by the IRS for employee benefits. As a financial planner, I have to keep an open mind to all potential techniques and not bring in my own personal preferences. Jack, I'm sorry to lecture you."

Jack smiled weakly. "Arthur, I'm sorry I tried to blow you off. I can see you have a lot more knowledge than other so-called financial planners Alex has tried to work with."

I shook Jack's hand and allowed my face to soften into a smile.

[5] *See Glossary, 13.*

"Jack, I'll probably be back after I talk to everyone. Let's try to work together to get this accounting on an audit-proof track. I will talk to Alex about my concerns."

"I agree. This is a good time to clean up this accounting mess. I'll outline some solutions before we meet again, but I need Alex's support. Since you'll be meeting with Gibby, please be careful. He is very dangerous." By the time I left, I knew we were both exhausted.

20

CHAPTER FOUR

Alex Revisited

As I drove up US-27 to return to the Grove, I thought about the events of the day. If I drank, and I don't, I would need a drink after the interview with Jack. Now I had to talk to Alex. I had no idea of how she would react. Thank goodness a local storm had come up and cooled things down. I felt a pleasant breeze. There was a wisp of coolness to the air, almost like fall was coming. I could get used to this small town atmosphere—no hurry, no worry. But I'm not sure I could handle the lack of privacy.

That night on the veranda I reviewed the facts with Alex. I watched her closely as I talked. Her eyes drooped a little, and her shoulders slumped as if she felt responsible…and very tired.

"Arthur, don't you think I know? As long as there is enough money to keep the Grove running, I close my eyes and let Jack write the checks. I sign whatever he gives me."

I am always amazed when seemingly intelligent clients get sucked in by others. Certainly Alex realized that her children were taking advantage of her.

"Alex, you understand that whatever plan I come up with will probably cut your children out of the cookie jar, don't you?"

"Arthur, let me tell you about my children. Tom wanted children, but I didn't. While Tom was alive, he kept them busy with sports and other activities. Somehow, for me the kids always took a back seat to the Grove, and they knew it. When Tom died, I couldn't—or wouldn't—fill the void he left. It has been all downhill since. I tried to make it up to the kids with money, but that hasn't worked."

It was nice sitting on the veranda. The heat had been oppressive during the day, but the breeze was delightful. Alex told me the long history of her family and the Grove, her father, and Tom. This had been a tough evening for Alex, but she seemed relieved now that I knew the truth. I felt I needed to switch our conversation to a more pleasant topic before the evening ended. I wanted to end on a good note.

"Alex, do you enjoy being a grandmother? Tell me about your two grandchildren."

Her demeanor immediately changed. Enthusiasm and pride showed in her eyes and her smile.

"You know, Arthur, I was amazed when Cindy had two children early in her marriage. They're away right now with their father, Cindy's ex. He is a good man who loves his children. Luckily, we're still friends. Typically, the kids are either with him, with me, or in school. Cindy has no use for them, and they know it. They love being at the Grove. They might change, but for right now they are a joy."

It was nice to see Alex had some joy in her life. She deserved it. My financial planning brain clicked in.

"Have you done any planning for them?" I queried.

"Yes, I put the maximum into two 529 college saving plans. I'm the owner, and my investment advisor handles the investments. Cindy doesn't even know the plans exist," she said.

I made a mental note of that. I'd add it to my notebook later.

"Who is the advisor?"

"Jackie Smith," she said.

This was a name I hadn't heard before. Maybe she was a little more ethical than other people in Alex's life. I could only hope.

"May I have the latest quarterly statement for your personally owned investments and the 529 plans? I want to look them over tonight."

"Are you going to have to see Jackie?"

"I don't think the investments are the issue here. The issue is the Grove."

I couldn't wait any longer. I tried to conceal my excitement, but I needed to energize myself. All this financial hide-and-seek had drained me. I was afraid Alex would consider my request juvenile, but I took a chance.

"Alex, may I see the trains?"

If my curiosity bothered Alex, she didn't show it.

"There's a room that was used by my father. I have a few of the trains in there. The rest are in storage."

I didn't even try to hide my giddiness. I had remembered to bring a standard catalog of Lionel trains. Since the trains had their original packaging, it would be easy to identify the type of train. My catalog had prices, so I could give Alex some idea of their value. This was my reward at the end of a long, hard day.

"Arthur, I pulled out one old train and a few that aren't quite as old," she said as I followed her to the back of the house.

Alex was obviously unaware of my excitement. She opened the door to a small office crowded with books and a very large desk. My eyes were drawn to a pile of file folders—and to what was sitting on top of it. The old train was in mint condition and was a 6 Type III locomotive. It had "Pennsylvania" stamped on the side. The "like new" price from the catalog was $1,900. I was afraid to touch it. Although Alex didn't know the exact date of purchase, I knew that Lionel produced these from 1906 through 1923.

"Alex, how many of these trains do you have?" I asked, barely able to contain myself.

"I think there are about ten or twelve with various other cars and pieces of equipment."

I assured her that seeing these few trains would be enough for me tonight. I enjoyed looking at the other pieces she had out. The other two locomotives in boxes were slightly newer 384 and 390 series from the 1930s. Alex took one of the loco-motives out of its box. She spoke quietly as she held it.

"My father displayed this one on his desk since I was a lit-tle girl. He liked this one the best. He ran the trains at Christmas around the tree and down the hall."

I was still afraid to touch anything. My hands were clasped behind my back just in case I couldn't control myself any longer.

"This one looks like a 392. Does it have a box?"

"Yes, it's in storage." Alex looked slightly amused. I guess the little kid in me was apparent. I bent even closer for a bet-ter look and nearly lost my balance. Now *that* would have been a disaster.

"The 392 is probably worth around $2,000. There were var-ious 392 models from the mid-1930s. Alex, will you consider selling them to me?"

Alex smiled, "Yes, but with one stipulation."

I knew it. This was too good to be true. I was afraid to hear the stipulation.

"What's that?"

"You can't sell them to anyone, and I want to know what will happen to them when you die. They would need to go someplace where other train collectors and kids could enjoy them."

I immediately had a plan. I hoped my idea would satisfy Alex's stipulation.

"How about this proposal? I'll buy them, and when I die, they will go to a museum. There is a museum in the old train depot in Naples, Florida. In the back of the depot, there's a train layout. The trains could go to a variety of similar museums around the country. I have seen many old train depots that have been turned into museums with train layouts."

"Will you run the trains?" Alex seemed to genuinely care about the trains and the enjoyment they were meant to provide.

"They will all run at Christmas. I have a big permanent layout."

Alex seemed pleased to hear this. "They need a good home where they will be appreciated. My children and grandchildren would just sell them when I die."

Yes, I could buy these trains on the open market, but I probably would never know who owned and loved them. I needed to find out more about Alex's father over the next day or two. She definitely was a daddy's girl. So far, she hadn't said anything about her mother.

As I went up to my room for the night, my thoughts switched to Alex's financial problem. I needed to sleep on it. All I had so far was raw data. During our conversation, Alex had told me there was a back road into the Grove. Apparently Orlando development was as close as that back road. I needed to see all of her land. Maybe a section of it could be sold to create liquidity. I began thinking about how the IRS would value the land. IRS would want to apply "best use" to the valuation, and the 3Ds would want to sell quickly. Estate taxes might take 40+ percent. Alex told me she had about $5 million in high quality investments and $5 million in life insurance. That was hardly enough liquidity to settle the estate taxes.

I wasn't kidding about the publicly traded company possibly being interested, but maybe selling the land along US-27 and the land along the back road to Orlando could reduce the Grove acreage and create more liquidity. Too bad the land wasn't closer to the university; the "ag" school would die for it. I might need to approach the university. Regardless, I had to keep all possible planning options open.

I decided that in the morning, before I went to see Alex's insurance agent, I would outline some alternatives. Harry's idea that this problem could be resolved in a day or two was not realistic. I imagined that I'd be staying with Alex for at least a week. I had to get used to non air-conditioned sleeping before one of the nights turned calm and sultry. At least it had cooled off by the time I went to sleep.

CHAPTER FIVE

Death

The sound of the birds woke me. I put the pillow over my head, but it didn't block out the sound. I'd had a restless night and would welcome more sleep, but it was no use. Reluctantly, I got up. I dressed casually. The air had turned humid by morning. I expected a hot, uncomfortable day. Although there wasn't a cloud in the sky, I knew it would rain. As I entered the kitchen, I noticed that it was like Alex, scantly decorated. There was a light breeze filtering through the open windows. Goldie looked up when I entered.

"Good morning, Goldie. What's for breakfast?"

"Miss Alex likes a lot of fruit and cereal. We are fortunate to have orange, grapefruit, banana, and avocado trees on the property. In the cooler months, Miss Alex has a big vegetable garden down by the lake," Goldie responded.

Goldie set a bowl of fresh fruit on the table. Several cereal boxes were already out. A pitcher of milk and vanilla yogurt completed the breakfast menu. I wasted no time making my cereal selection and scooping fresh fruit atop it. I had just begun to eat when Alex entered.

"Good morning, Alex. This fruit is delicious."

At first I thought she was wearing the same simple clothes she wore last night, but then realized these seemed more worn.

I expected her to go out and work the back forty with a horse and plow. She had a nice glow to her skin. She looked healthy, but then again it might have been from her high blood pressure.

"Did you sleep ok last night? There was a nice breeze, but it was sultry. Going to storm today. I can feel it in my bones," Alex asked.

"Truthfully, Alex, I've become soft. When I first came to Florida, I lived without air conditioning, but now I can't. I'll get used to the heat in a day or two."

Alex laughed. "All Floridians are soft. You're not alone."

Alex spent little time eating a bowl of fruit and drinking a glass of juice.

"Arthur, how about going for a walk? I always walk around one part of the Grove each morning."

Ah, the perfect opportunity. I could get some exercise, see the land, and find out some more information.

"Sounds good. I have more questions," I remarked.

She gave me a dubious look...as if I couldn't possibly have any questions left. "I thought you asked every imaginable question last night."

"Sorry, my questions this morning will be personal."

Alex and I left the house and walked into the small backyard. We weren't far from US-27, but I couldn't see or hear the traffic because the house was surrounded by orange trees. Engulfed might be a more accurate word. We followed the dirt road that cut through the neat rows of orange trees until we came to a narrow road that led into town. We had been walking uphill. I walked out of the orange trees, stood beside the road, and looked toward Orlando. I could see the roofs of a housing development in the distance. Alex wanted to show me that Orlando development was at her back door. We had a long

28

walk back to the house. I asked Alex if she'd mind answering some questions as we walked.

"Ok, what do you want to know?"

"Alex, you look in great shape. Do you have any medical issues?" I queried.

"The doctors have warned me that my blood pressure medicine is just barely keeping my blood pressure under control. I am not supposed to lose my temper. That's one reason that I like to take a walk each morning—being out among the trees has a calming effect."

I'd have to be careful that the personal questions—and the financial planning I was thinking about suggesting—didn't make her lose her temper. I certainly didn't want to be blamed for causing a heart attack!

"Good God, here I am asking you questions. Please understand I'm just here to help you. Are you ready for some tough questions?"

"May I answer them honestly?" I felt as if Alex was warning me that her answers may be as tough to handle as were my questions.

"Absolutely. Have you ever been approached by the big orange harvest or juice companies to sell the Grove? Exchanging your stock for publicly traded stock would clear the estate liquidity problem your family will be facing."

Alex paused before responding.

"I was approached a few years ago, but I suspected that immediately after the exchange, the Grove would be bulldozed. Arthur, do you realize that developers want this land for little other than housing? This spine of Florida has dirt that can be sold. Then they'll level this land flatter than a pancake."

I grimaced, imagining another cookie cutter development, devoid of all trees. Then I persisted. My argument had to be convincing enough to change her mind. "How about closing a deal that would guarantee the Grove would remain unchanged for twenty to thirty years?"

Alex seemed to soften a little. For the first time, I noticed a hint of resignation—almost defeat.

"I might be interested," she replied. "I am tired of making all the day-to-day decisions. This is a big piece of property."

"So you aren't opposed to this idea?"

"Tell me more," she said.

"How about setting up a charitable trust to benefit the university with the land?"

"Arthur, as much as my children dislike me and as much as I would like to donate the land to the university, my kids and grandkids need income."

"You mean, $5-$10 million each isn't enough to satisfy them?" I tried to hide my sarcasm, but I'm pretty sure Alex picked up on it.

"You're right, but I just can't give it away."

"How about a bargain sale with the university?"[6] I asked.

"How would that work?"

I explained. "Well, let's make it simple. Let's say we take a portion worth $10 million and sell it to the university for $5 million. Five million is a charitable gift, and $5 million is a sale subject to capital gains tax. Jack would have to do some tax number crunches because of recapture possibilities, but I don't want to start him looking at income and estate savings if you are opposed to the idea."

"Sounds interesting," Alex said.

"I understand you have some life insurance in trust. Tell me about that."

"Well, after Tom died, I knew my children would face the same estate liquidity problems I had when my parents died. I bought $5 million worth. I was only mildly hypertensive then.

[6] *See Glossary, 2.*

The policy had a small rating. I thought the policy would cover the estate tax, but then the real estate took off."

"Did you try to buy more?" I asked.

"Yes, I applied for additional life insurance a few years ago, but the premium was excessive, so I didn't buy the policy. In addition, about that time the original life insurance policy premium went up by 50%," Alex explained.

"Why?"

"The agent said the interest rates weren't guaranteed. The policy got into trouble with low interest rates in 2001 through 2004."

"I need to see the policy," I said.

I knew that universal life policies had earning problems with the low interest rates.[7] I bet the original proposal illustrated higher interest rates.

"My attorney has it," Alex said, "but the agent has all the information."

"I planned to see your agent this morning. I'll stop by his office to see if I can figure this out."

"So you are going into town?"

"Let's call the agent to make sure he'll be in. And, I need authorization from you to review all of your policies including your life insurance," I explained.

"If he can see you, please do me a favor, Arthur. Take Goldie into town with you. She has a hair appointment this morning. Try not to intimidate the insurance agent like you did Jack. People are kind of laid back around here. Word gets around fast."

"That quick?" I said.

"Yep."

On the way to town, Goldie talked freely about how Alex's parents had taken her in after her parents died. Goldie had

---

[7] *See Glossary, 24.*

worked at the Grove for forty years. Her affection for Alex was obvious. She admired Alex's straightforward and easygoing manner with the Grove crew and with her. Even though Alex was almost ten years older, Goldie thought of her as a sister.

I asked her why she never got married. Her answer surprised me.

"I was married. I married one of the Grove workers years ago. It gets sort of slow in the summer, so one year he took a temporary job up North and never came back. I don't even know if he is alive. But I'm okay. I have a great life with Alex and her grandchildren," Goldie replied.

"What about her children?"

"They are only interested in Alex's money. Less than worthless, all three of them. The only time they come around is for money. Alex got so disgusted with them that her CPA, Jack, handles all money matters now."

"Yes, I found out yesterday how they are raiding the cookie jar. Can't wait to meet them," I said sarcastically.

Goldie rolled her eyes.

"Oh, they know you're here, and after what I heard over the breakfast table, Jack is spreading the word. Alex likes you because you are no-nonsense. The other financial planners that came around were only after her money. I hope you can help her."

"Is this the beauty shop?"

"In this town, there is only one."

"I'll pick you up in an hour or so."

"That'll be fine, Arthur. Thank you."

I left Goldie and headed for the insurance agent's office. Sam Waters, the insurance agent, had a professional looking office on Main Street. I noticed he was an independent agent. Although I don't sell insurance any more, I was an insurance agent for thirty years as part of my financial planning practice. In addition, I've done some expert witness work, mainly on the plaintiff side. I know where sleeping dogs lie for both investments and insurance cases.

I opened the building door. Another blast of cold air hit me. "Hi, I'm Arthur. Is Mr. Waters in?"

"He will be with you in a minute. He's on the phone right now. May I get you a cup of coffee or a soda?" the receptionist asked politely.

"No, I am ok right now, thanks."

I sat down and looked around me. It wasn't a large office—the desks were crowded together. Sam had about six or seven people working in the office. Besides life insurance, he sold auto, homeowners, and business insurance. I thought I would loosen him up with questions about the crop insurance. I thought that might catch him off guard since he probably was ready only for the life insurance questions. Plus, I already knew what had happened to the universal life insurance policies over the past ten years or so. I wasn't that interested in her existing policy but with what happened with the second policy Alex recently applied for. I had to figure out her potential life expectancy. The door to the only private office opened. A short, stocky man bounced toward me and grabbed my hand.

"Hi, Arthur, I'm Sam Waters. Welcome to small town USA." Sam continued to pump my hand up and down. I could see he was trying to overwhelm me with his personality. I extricated my hand from Sam's grasp. Sam directed me to his glass-enclosed office.

"This is a neat little town, Sam, but I don't see it staying small for too long. The housing market will turn around. This area is prime for development and, because it's inland, homeowners insurance is still affordable."

"You're right about that. So how can I help you?"

"Well, I want to talk to you about Alex's lack of crop insurance. Not having crop insurance cost her a bundle."

Sam was visibly taken aback. I was right. I had definitely caught him off guard.

"The crop insurance?"

"Yes. Is there something wrong? You did propose it, didn't you?"

"Gee, I guess so. I don't know."

I found it hard to believe that he couldn't remember whether or not he had proposed purchasing crop insurance. Was he hiding something?

"Well, how about pulling your file. You handle Alex's other insurance for the home and the Grove, don't you?"

"Yes, but I didn't think we would be talking about her other insurance."

"Why not? A good financial planner always reviews all the client's risks. I also want to see how much liability coverage she has. You can sort of see the lake from US-27. I'm afraid some kids could cut through the Grove to the lake. Who knows what might happen."

"Listen, Arthur, I'm not sure I can show you the files."

Again I sensed that something was amiss. Why was Sam stalling?

"But Alex already authorized you to show me *all* of her policies."

"What do you know about insurance? You're a financial planner."

Just like Jack from yesterday, I thought to myself. People don't understand that good financial planners have to know about all aspects of planning.

"I've got news for you, Sam. I was a life, health, and property-casualty agent for thirty years. Although I'm not currently active, I keep my insurance license so that I can teach continuing education courses. The course I like to teach most is ethics. Let's see the files."

The bad news was that in order to keep a competitive price in Florida's rising insurance market, Sam had cut Alex's liability protection to a basic $1 million for the Grove. Even worse, he had never proposed crop insurance. In fact, she told me she had asked about it, and he didn't recommend it. A perfect plaintiff's case.

My invasive questions did loosen him up. Mission accomplished. It was time now to shift gears to the real reason for my visit. Before I could begin, a bolt of lightning hit nearby, and Sam jumped a foot. In a few minutes, the heavens opened up. I could tell this was going to be a monster of a storm, so I settled into my chair. There was no going outside now.

"Sam, since I have some time now, I want to talk about Alex's $5 million life insurance policy," I said.

His head jerked. Instead of asking the staff to get the file, like he had for my previous request, he left the room to get it himself. He returned in a few minutes with the file in hand. I went over the original illustration and projections. There was nothing unusual about the policy. He had applied to six major life insurance carriers to get the best policy. After the attorney had drawn the trust, the application was signed by the trustee, Alex's attorney. The beneficiary was the trust. Everything appeared to be in order; however, even if I can't find something wrong, I ask questions.

The application contained the medical information from the physical performed by the insurance approved doctor. The medical application had her blood pressure, weight, and her personal physician information. Unfortunately, the personal physician Attending Physician Statement (APS) wasn't in the file. I proceeded to ask questions about underwriting, the carriers, and the rating. I really wanted to read her medical information. Getting to her actual files at her doctor's office might prove difficult, and I needed to know now, not two or three months from now. I really needed to know more about her health than this told me.

I felt hopeless. From what I could tell, everything was in order. As an expert witness, I am trained to snoop. Although we were still in the midst of a violent thunderstorm, the air conditioning had cooled the building down to a point where I was cold. Yet, Sam was noticeably sweating. I got the feeling that something was being hidden from me. There was nothing else I could think of, so I switched gears.

"Sam, what about the second application?" I thought he was going to have a heart attack. "You ok, Sam? I want to talk about her trying to get more life insurance coverage. She said the policy was too expensive."

This line of questioning seemed to calm him down. He explained that her blood pressure and personal physician's report were so bad that four of the six companies said "Thanks, but no thanks." The other two companies proposed premiums that indicated she had less than a ten-year life expectancy. The carriers were major players in the substandard life insurance market. I knew I had him on the ropes, but I was out of questions, and I couldn't find anything wrong. I asked him again for the file with the second application. Sam blurted out that he hadn't kept the file because Alex hadn't accepted the policy. I knew I needed to ask Alex more about her health history. Unfortunately, her parents had died in an auto accident, and she probably knew nothing about their health.

"Sam, thanks for all the information. Looks like the storm is about over. I might have additional questions after I see Alex's attorney this afternoon."

Sam gave another noticeable jerk with my last comment. Something in the policy wasn't right. Sam shouldn't be surprised that Alex's attorney was the trustee—especially with three worthless kids.

I said goodbye and left to pick up Goldie. Frankly, I never expected to unearth any planning opportunities with Sam. I figured Alex to be uninsurable with her health issues. But Sam was uneasy about the life insurance questions. It wasn't like the $5 million policy would be cancelled or replaced by another policy. In fact, the original carrier would lose money on the policy because of Alex's shortened life expectancy. Goldie was waiting for me when I pulled up.

"Arthur, that was quite a storm. The trees will be washed clean. I can't wait to get back to the Grove. Everything will smell fresh."

With Goldie directing me, we drove back down the old grove roads. This was what old Florida looked like before the land developers. We turned into the Grove and followed the dirt road back to the house. By now the storm had moved west. With the sun to the east, only the top of the cloud remained. I told Goldie the cloud in the sky looked like a dead head.

She laughed, "Arthur, you might have some country in you yet."

"What do you mean by that?" I wondered.

"That's an old country expression for what remains of the clouds after a thunderstorm has passed."

Goldie was silent for a moment.

"Most people, including Floridians, wouldn't stay at the house overnight. If Alex doesn't like someone, she'll ask them to join her in the hottest room in the house. She won't even turn on the fan. Within minutes they are mopping their face while she's as cool as a cucumber. They don't stay long, and they don't come back. Alex and I have a good laugh after they leave. I knew she was interested in you when you two had lunch and dinner on the veranda with the fan on."

She continued, "Alex and Harry have been friends since college. Harry and Alex dated before Alex met Tom. Afterwards, Alex and Harry remained friends. Harry's saying you are the best was good enough for Alex."

"I appreciate Harry's trust, but I still haven't found a solution to her situation. He won't continue to sing my praises if I can't help Alex."

The storm had bathed the trees, and they did sparkle. All traces of tire tracks had disappeared. The sandy soil was like Daytona Beach, flat and hard. When we arrived at the house, all was quiet. The electricity appeared to be off. As we entered through the screen door, Goldie called out to Alex.

"Alex, we're back."

There was no response. Goldie had mentioned that Alex often goes out in the Grove after a downpour to check any washouts due to the hilly nature of the land. While Goldie checked for Alex in the kitchen, I went into the living room. I have been around death as an insurance agent, as a financial planner, and as a family member. I will never get used to it.

Alex was lying face down on the carpet in the living room. Her clothes were unchanged from our morning breakfast and walk. I checked her pulse and felt her arm. Her body was already cooling. The toughest part was telling Goldie. Goldie insisted on checking herself and then disappeared into her room. I wasn't sure what to do, so I called the Sheriff. I figured the Sheriff would help me make the right decision.

At first I didn't think the Sheriff heard me. Seconds passed before he spoke in a trembling voice.

"You're sure she's dead?"

"I'm sure. No pulse. Rigor mortis has started," I said.

"I'm still sending EMS, and I'll be there in ten minutes. I doubt EMS will beat me there, but if they do, don't let anyone touch or move anything."

"What?" But he had hung up. Within minutes I heard the sirens. EMS and the Sheriff arrived in a dead heat. The Sheriff must have goosed EMS because the two EMS guys ran into the house with the Sheriff. It took them about one minute to verify my diagnosis, and then the EMS guys were gone.

"Who the hell are you? Where is Goldie? Did you touch or move anything? What are you doing here?" the Sheriff asked.

"Hold on, Sheriff. Let me answer. You've got to calm down. I know about your relationship with Alex."

He looked distraught.

"What the hell?"

"My name is Arthur. I'm a financial planner. I came here to work with Alex. Goldie is in her room. She's been there since we found Alex."

"Arthur who?"

"No, my last name is Arthur. I think you know Harry Blackstone. He sent me. You can check me out."

I was sure that the Sheriff knew Harry. Harry had visited the Grove many times. He had never given up his attraction to Alex. The Sheriff wasn't messing around; he called some crime specialists and the coroner's office. He asked me some basic questions. Then he went to the back of the house to get Goldie. While I was waiting for them to return, I could think only of Alex's morning calmness. Now she was dead due to an apparent heart attack.

When they returned, I heard the Sheriff ask Goldie if she saw anything out of place. Goldie slowly walked around the body and the room. She opened and closed a table drawer. I realized she knew exactly where every dust particle should be. She had gone from being distressed to totally focused. The Sheriff knew what he was doing.

Finally she spoke. "Sheriff, someone was here."

"What makes you say that?" he asked.

"The gun in that drawer is facing in the wrong direction. Although that drawer is closed, the gun is opposite. Alex was right-handed, and the gun is placed left-handed. The gun has been out or moved, and someone else put it back. Secondly, the nitro tablets are right there. Why didn't she take one? Lastly, there is a bruise on her right hand," Goldie explained.

The Sheriff said, "Goldie, the bruise could be from being out in the Grove."

"Well, maybe, but I've never seen her as calm as she was this morning. She believed that Arthur was here to help her. When he and I left for town, she told me she was going to think about what Arthur had said. The grove workers just finished cleaning and fertilizing the trees. Alex supervised. Nothing else had to be done. She even said she would have lunch ready for us when we returned. There was no bruise."

"Anything else?" he asked.

"No, but if she died of a heart attack, someone caused it. Sheriff, if I think of something else, I'll let you know. Meantime, being in this room is too much for me," she said sadly.

Once again Goldie retreated to the back of the house. I was worried about her.

When the crime scene personnel came, they took my fingerprints. They checked the front door and the only fingerprints were mine. It almost appeared that the door handle had been wiped clean. Since the doors and windows were never locked, no other evidence was found.

After everyone left and the body was taken for an autopsy, the Sheriff sat down. He motioned me to sit near him. I could see he was trying to make his mind up about something.

"You have a first name, Arthur?"

"Yes, I'll tell you if you need to know," I said.

"No. It isn't important. Look, after what Goldie said, I am suspicious. However, I expect that after the autopsy, nothing will be found. Someone caused her to lose her temper or threatened her. She may have tried to reach for the gun, but whoever it was caught her hand in the drawer. When she couldn't get to the nitro, it was all over in a matter of minutes."

"Sounds plausible to me, but how do you prove it, and who did it?"

"You're exactly right, Arthur. Besides her three worthless children, there are at least two land developers who would like to see her dead. I understand you put the fear of God in Jack yesterday. This is a small town, and she is a big landowner. You may have caused her death."

His last sentence really hit home. I can be a real bad ass as an expert witness. I may have won some big settlement financial planning lawsuits, but none of my clients had died. The Sheriff saw the look of despair on my face.

"Listen, Arthur, I didn't mean that the way it came out."

"You might be right."

"Well, one thing is for sure. I need your help to flush out the killer," he said.

I'm sure my shock showed on my face. I gulped for air, then blurted out my first thought.

"This is out of my league!" I exclaimed.

"You worried someone here in town. Maybe you can help me find out who it is. I want you to stay around town and see what you can find out. You're working for me now."

"Well, it wasn't her insurance agent. He was with me."

I thought for a moment.

"What's my justification? I don't have a client anymore. Everyone will shut down and wait the storm out."

"No, you're going to work for the Sheriff's department. I'm going to make sure that the death certificate isn't issued and that word gets out that her death was a possible homicide."

I thought to myself, "This is something new—I'm supposed to be investigating a homicide. I'm not sure how I feel about all this."

"How much do you make per hour, Arthur?"

"You don't want to know, Sheriff." I paused and then continued, "Sheriff, I have never walked away from anything I've started. I do feel responsible. Harry will never forgive me when he finds out about this. As fast as this happened, and with a limited potential murderers' pool, my prediction is that something will turn up in a day or two. I have already questioned two people, so all I have left are her three children and her attorney. Anyone else come to mind?"

"No. Since the building boom is in a bust cycle, the land developers are licking their wounds. They wouldn't want to take on a property of this magnitude."

The Sheriff paused for a moment.

"If you don't mind, I would like you to stay here at the house with Goldie. She doesn't have anywhere to go, and the nearest decent motel is twenty minutes away."

Before the Sheriff left, he shared background on his relationship with Alex. He met Alex the night her parents died in an auto accident. He was a Sheriff's deputy on duty when the call came in that there was a head-on crash on US-27. A drunk had turned on the wrong side of the road. During the investigation, he met Alex. After he became Sheriff, their paths crossed occasionally. A few years after Tom's death, they met at a Fourth of July fireworks display in town. He asked if he could see her. A year later she said yes. He had a failed marriage, and she wasn't interested in getting married again, so they did simple things together including enjoying a sexual relationship. Hardly anyone knew about it because Alex kept to herself and wasn't very social. Since the house isn't visible from the road, no one ever saw his sheriff's car there.

"Arthur, because of this relationship, I don't want my people investigating Alex's death. Some people around here who don't like me as Sheriff might use this against me at the next election. You know everything about the relationship, and I was meeting with the town council all morning, so you know that I didn't do it."

"Sheriff, you didn't have to tell me that."

"Yes, I did. I needed to clear the air about myself. You can check on that."

The Sheriff moved toward the door. Before he left, he turned to face me.

"How are you going to start?" he asked.

"I think it would be a good idea if you called Alex's attorney and arranged a morning meeting. He isn't likely to talk to me unless you tell him to. You are going to have to tell him that it's a possible homicide and that I'm working for you. Even though he is Alex's attorney, his mouth will wag. This will get around quickly," I replied.

"Arthur, you could really work for the Sheriff's department if your current occupation doesn't pan out."

"No thanks, Sheriff. I'm out of my element."

"We'll see. You need anything, call me. My office will find me. If we find out who did this, they'd better give up peacefully because I will kill him or her or them and call it self defense."

CHAPTER SIX

Goldie

About dinner time, Goldie came out of her room. She looked fragile—almost lifeless.

"Arthur, I'm cooking dinner. Please don't argue with me."

I knew she needed to stay busy rather than sitting alone in her room.

"All right, Goldie, but keep it simple. I'm not letting you eat alone. Let's sit out on the front porch, not the veranda," I said calmly.

To my surprise, Goldie spent the next hour preparing country fried steak with all the fixings. She moved around the kitchen like a robot. At dinner, we talked about Alex's parents. They had treated her like a daughter, and Alex had treated her like a sister. I sensed that Goldie needed some assurance about her situation. So I lied a little.

"I talked to the Sheriff. He wants me to stay on to investigate Alex's death. I need someplace to stay and someone to take care of me. So I'm staying here for the time being. In the meantime, the Sheriff is going to check around for you. He said he knows two or three families that need a housekeeper."

"Arthur, that's nice of you and the Sheriff to look after me. I'll take care of you. But I need you to help me with another

44

matter. I'd like to hire you as a financial planner. I know I can trust you if Alex did."

I wasn't sure where Goldie was going with this conversation, but I listened closely.

"I never made very much working for Alex, but I never spent anything. Alex helped me invest what I earned. I have about $2 million, and I think Alex may have included me in her will," Goldie said.

"It will be my pleasure to help you, Goldie."

I would have never guessed. It was the millionaire-next-door story.

"However, for right now I need a good base and someone I can talk to. The only people I trust are you and the Sheriff. After we solve Alex's death, then we will both be able to concentrate on your situation," I said.

As a financial planner, I had learned over the years that potential clients with fancy cars usually didn't have a penny to their names. They were all flash and no financial substance. Goldie caught me off guard. Although not rich, she was probably set for retirement with $2 million and Social Security. Clients who don't overspend in their preretirement years generally don't change their habits in retirement. Working a plan for her would be interesting. I knew one thing for sure; she wasn't going to work again. Her working life was over.

I went to bed too early and sleep came hard. I tossed and turned and was up and down three times during the night. Before dawn I was dressed and eager to begin my day. Walking quietly through the house, I headed out to the Grove. The Grove was a mature orange grove. I knew that these trees were doomed, and it saddened me. I had been driving up US-27 north of I-4 to see clients in the 1970s and 1980s. The groves had stretched from I-4 north to Clermont and beyond. In Clermont, they had a citrus tower. You could go up inside it to see the trees for miles around. A couple of acts of nature and the trees north of I-4 were gone. The weather was cold for too long in the 1980s. As an interesting side note to the freeze, the airline pilots knew about the severity of the weather and bought orange juice futures. Those that bought made big money. Now on this morning, I wanted to grab onto these trees to save them for future generations. But I had no hope. I didn't have the power to save them for the future. After a long walk, I returned to the house. Goldie already had breakfast waiting.

"Arthur, I heard you get up and leave. I couldn't stay in bed this morning either. I feel awful, like I have a hangover," she said in a tired voice.

"Goldie, we can only stay at the house a day or two at the most. The Sheriff says he is going to delay the funeral as long as possible by not releasing Alex's body. He wants to keep the tension up. My job is to tighten the screws. Can you think of anything else that might be important?"

"Arthur, it has to be one of the kids. I know that Alex wasn't the perfect mother. The two girls were intimidated by their mother's dynamic personality. Alex was like some TV movie; she was the family matriarch. She was bigger than life. Don't believe anything those kids tell you. Who are you seeing first?"

"I have a 9:00 A.M. appointment with Adam Sanders. What do you know about him?" I asked.

"After Alex's parents died and all the IRS problems, Alex and Tom did some basic planning. Tom's father and Adam's father were fraternity brothers."

"How did Alex and Adam get along?"

"Well, when Tom died, Adam handled Tom's estate. It was pretty easy because almost everything came back to Alex. I think about $600,000 went into trust for the children. They only get income from the trust because the money stays in the trust until the kids die and then the remainder passes to Alex's grandchildren," Goldie explained.

"That sounds like good basic planning."

"Arthur, what you need to know is that Adam and Gibby are drinking buddies."

"So Adam handles that $600,000 trust, apparently the life insurance trust, and the trust with the Grove property. Interesting," I said warily.

"Because Adam knows that when Alex dies, Gibby will inherit the control of all of the assets, he is going to be cagey with you. What kind of information do you expect to get out of Adam?"

"I have no experience with this type of investigation. There's no indication that he had anything to do with Alex's death—only that Adam represents her estate. I don't even have a letter authorizing me to represent her. But I think the Sheriff may have threatened Adam. Seems like the Sheriff knows where the dirt is buried around here. Given the Sheriff's mood, I doubt Adam will refuse to see me."

Having this conversation was tough. Goldie and I were depressed by Alex's death, and Goldie was still visibly shaken by the shock of it all. I asked her if there was anything I could bring back from town. She shook her head slowly back and forth.

"What are you doing today, Goldie?" I asked.

I didn't want her spending the day in her room.

"Arthur, there's only one thing that might distract me a bit. I'm going to clean."

I sat at the table for a few moments, trying to gather my energy. I would much rather get in my car and head toward Tampa than toward town.

CHAPTER SEVEN

Adam

As I drove, I thought about my situation. A small Florida town, the Sheriff, a murder...it all felt like something from the past. A time warp was the best way to describe it. As I parked my car in front of Adam's office, a burly man emerged from the shadows. It had to be Gibby. Since he was about twice my size, I decided I might as well get out and try to act friendly.

"Hi, you must be Gibby. My name is Arthur."

Since he didn't extend his hand for me to shake, I didn't extend mine. I wasn't sure I would get it back in one piece. Gibby looked like he hadn't slept all night, and his breath was foul. Nothing good was going to come of this.

"Get out of town before I run you out of town," he said, trying to be threatening.

The words came out hard and without any inflection. Gibby was a sleep-deprived drunk. He looked like he had been up all night drinking and then had been stewing in the hot morning sun. Even though it was morning, the temperature was already 90° in the shade with 100% humidity (normal Florida weather).

"Gibby, I understand that you're upset over your mother's death, but you need to calm down and get some sleep."

I really didn't know what to say to Gibby. I certainly didn't trust his judgement in his present condition. And I wasn't ready for a brawl.

"If you hadn't come into town, my mother wouldn't have died of a heart attack. She would still be alive," Gibby said in a rant.

"Gibby, how do you know she died of a heart attack?"

"Listen, you son-of-a-bitch, it's all around town that the Sheriff put you up to making this into a homicide."

So the Sheriff was right. The homicide probability had spread with the midnight air. When I didn't react to Gibby and started for Adam's office, Gibby bolted and blocked my way. Still, I didn't react. I didn't know what to do or say next. I learned a long time ago that sometimes it's better to keep your mouth shut. Gibby was about to implode.

"I guess you didn't hear me. If you don't get your ass out of town, you'll spend the next six months in the hospital."

Still no reaction on my part. Gibby was a physical bruiser. I'm no wimp, but I was not a match for him. We had been in the hot sun for about ten minutes. Between his temper and the temperature, his skin had the look of boiled shrimp. I just stood there. I figured I could take the hot sun; he couldn't.

Something had to happen. It did. Gibby pulled a gun out of his waistband that had been hidden by his hanging gut. I hate guns. I was at a loss as to what to do. Gibby pointed the gun at me. All of a sudden, his eyes shifted. A patrol car was slowly coming down the street. While he was distracted, I quickly jogged around him into Adam's office. My quick movement through the door startled the receptionist.

After I caught my breath, I said, "Miss, my name is Arthur. I have an appointment with Adam Sanders, but I need to use your phone first."

I called the Sheriff from a side office. I wasn't about to get myself killed. Most of my friends know I hate guns, but I am a crack shot. My vision is perfect. It took a few minutes to get the Sheriff on the line. But there was no doubt in my mind that the department took any call from me as serious and would get the Sheriff on the line wherever he was.

"Good morning, Arthur, what's the problem?"

"I hate to tell you, but your plan worked too well. Gibby was waiting for me in front of Adam's office," I said in a rush.

"Did he threaten you?" he asked.

"Yes, he pulled a gun on me."

"Wow, what happened?"

"Well, one of your cruisers came down the street. He was badly hung over, so the distraction was enough for me to get past him into Adam's office. Luckily, he didn't follow me in. Frankly, as hot as it is out, he'll turn into a boiled beet if he waits for me. Either way, I don't want to take him on when I leave," I explained.

"The only one who could have told Gibby you were coming is Adam."

Since I was standing near Adam's receptionist, all I could do was grunt. The Sheriff heard my grunt and understood. I had said as much as I wanted to say. Maybe even too much.

"Arthur, how long will you be at Adam's office?"

"Maybe an hour?"

"I'm sending a deputy. His name is Dale. From now on he'll be with you twenty-four hours a day. I have a feeling you are going to smoke someone out, and he or she may come after you. If Gibby knows, then everyone in town knows. Don't leave until Dale gets there," he said sternly.

"Don't worry. I won't!"

I had to wait a few minutes to see Adam. How much of the conversation he heard didn't matter. Hopefully, he notified

Gibby to stay away. I was shown to Adam's office by the receptionist. Since Adam didn't even stand up or shake my hand, I decided to get right to the point. Adam already knew why I was there, and he didn't look too happy. His tone was defensive and direct.

"Arthur, I'm the personal representative of Alex's estate. I have an attorney-client relationship. You wasted your time coming here. Even if you have a subpoena, I'm not going to release her documents," Adam said haughtily.

"I am not asking you to release the documents but to review them with me and answer some questions," I explained.

"I thought I already made my position clear."

A long time ago and in a different occupation, I learned a trick. Adam thought I was leaving and looked down. I was wearing my favorite shoes. They are twenty-five year-old wingtips, and the sole is about one-inch thick, tough as nails. As I got up, I kicked the middle leg of his desk as hard as I could. The leg had no chance, and the desk moved backwards. He almost jumped out of his seat. I had his attention. He attempted to say something, but I beat him to the punch.

"Why not call the Sheriff, Adam?"

He glared at me. I had him. I was sure he sent Gibby home and I knew Dale was coming.

"Adam, let me get to the point. You told Gibby I was coming. You are the only one who knew. The Sheriff didn't tell anyone else. I might have respected your attorney-client privilege before Gibby pulled a gun on me. Now, I'm going to get some answers."

"Go to hell."

I reached across the desk. His chair flew backwards, and I picked up his phone and started to dial the Sheriff.

"Who you calling?"

"The Sheriff. If you think I'm pissed, wait until he shows up. You know his relationship with Alex. He told me that if this is a homicide, the killer will never make it to jail."

Adam was visibly shaken. I, however, knew I was powerless. All he had to do was to wait me out. I decided to play my trump card.

"Fine, don't answer me. Play your attorney-client privilege. But I've got news for you. I know the top people at the life insurance carrier, and I'll call them to report a possible homicide. They can hold up the death benefit payment until the homicide issue is settled." I could be just as threatening.

That got his attention. Just like yesterday, there was something about this life insurance policy that made him sweat. Apparently, Adam and Gibby had been out drinking together. His sweat smelled like flat beer. He looked as if he hadn't slept much. One of my former clients had been accused of murdering his wife, so I knew what to expect, and so did Adam.

An insurer faces a problem when the insured is murdered and the named beneficiary is suspected, accused, or actually convicted of killing the insured.[8] Interestingly, the life insurance trust, not the person, was the owner-beneficiary.[9] In some cases, the insured's estate may challenge the primary beneficiary's right to recover. There is a common law principle that prohibits a beneficiary from benefiting from the life insurance policy proceeds when he or she kills the insured or commits a wrongful act that directly results in the insured's death.

Adam's reaction to my threat to contact the insurance carrier was almost inaudible.

"Why are you doing this?"

"Well, besides the Sheriff asking me to, no one seems saddened by Alex's death. From what I could see in my short time

[8] *See Glossary, 3.*
[9] *See Glossary, 14.*

with her, she was a person who should be missed. Neither Gibby nor you has said a kind word about her."

"My relationship with Alex started off okay but suffered when I started drinking with Gibby. I took Gibby's side on one minor issue, and Alex blew up. She threatened to fire me. She swore she'd go to the bar association if Gibby knew anything about her estate planning. Things got very tense. I assured her that Gibby and I are just friends and that I would never betray her trust. She didn't fire me, but she didn't send me any new business or referrals. The relationship grew very cold," Adam said.

"Listen, Adam. You can make both of our lives easier if we can go over the documents."

"Do you even know anything about trust documents?"

"I read them all the time for my clients, but I'm not an attorney and don't write documents."

"Well, these are really basic."

Adam relented, and together we began to review the documents. The first one was a will with a testamentary trust.[10] I thought with the Grove it would be a revocable trust.[11] I was surprised that it authorized Adam to sell the Grove to the highest bidder. Adam picked up on my surprised expression.

"Ok, before you ask me, Arthur, I'll answer you. You want to know why a testamentary rather than a revocable trust. This is going through probate court, and I will get some fees, but if you read on, I'll get a flat fee for selling the Grove. I believed it would be easier to sell the Grove if the asset wasn't in trust. I thought I could sell the asset faster, pay the IRS, and clear out the potential creditors. You will have to trust me; this is what Alex wanted. The remainderment goes into the testamentary trust with spendthrift provisions for the three children.[12] The children can't invade principal even for health reasons.

53

[10] *See Glossary, 21.*
[11] *See Glossary, 16.*
[12] *See Glossary, 19.*

Then, after the last of the children dies, the residue goes out-right to Alex's two grandchildren. In addition, Arthur, as you know, only certain trusts can hold S corporation stock. I did-n't want the stock to have to pass into a qualified subchapter S trust (QSST).[13] I think it's simpler to sell the Grove and then place the remaining assets in the testamentary trust. Then I sat, saying nothing. I was just about at the end of my law and document knowledge. Adam sensed that. He knew he had me.

The two documents, the will and the testamentary trust, were exactly as he explained. A bit unusual, but I didn't notice any red flags. The fee for handling the sale was unusual but very fair. I understood why Alex chose Adam as the executor. He could probably handle the probate court better than any of the family members. Normally, a trustee has to have skill in ongoing financial management. I found out he was already trustee of the $600,000 bypass trust set up at Tom's death.[14] Although the trust income was being paid out to the three children, Adam showed me that the trust assets had grown close to $1 million. He was very proud of his integrity and impartiality. I noticed that Jackie Smith was the investment advisor. I had reviewed Alex's investments the night before and found nothing out of the ordinary. A bit conservative for me, but not for Alex and apparently not for Adam.

The next document was a revocable trust.[15] All Alex's cash-type assets (such as investments) were in this trust. Alex really only owned two assets: the Grove and investments. I realized that the house was owned by the Grove. I couldn't resist. I had to ask Adam a question.

"Who gets Alex's personal property?" I asked.

"Well, there isn't much."

I wasn't sure how to broach the subject of the trains. Alex had been dead less than twenty-four hours, and I was con-

[13] See Glossary, 15.
[14] See Glossary, 5.
[15] See Glossary, 16.

cerned about my own interests. I realized I was being crass, but I had to know.

"This may sound stupid, Adam, but I came out here with a promise that Alex would sell me her old Lionel trains."

"I didn't know she had old trains."

"They were her father's trains."

"Are they valuable?"

"Relative to the other assets, no. But they are worth a total of about $10 to $20,000 dollars. I really only saw some of them," I replied.

"Well, they'll be part of her probate estate. I can let you bid on them."

Now that we got through this silly issue, Adam definitely looked more relaxed. I made a mistake asking about the trains. I lost my advantage. I became too personal. I regrouped and tried to put this conversation back on a business level.

"Do you know anything about the investments in the revocable trust Adam?" I asked.

"No, she has a broker in Orlando. That's all I know. I know the investment account is down after the Grove's expenses in the years 2005 and 2006 even though the market was good. Arthur, when you find out about the value of the investment, will you call me? I have to have some idea about her liquid assets."

Even though I knew how much was in the revocable trust investment account, I said, "I guess so, but who gets this money when the testamentary trust ends?"

"Her grandchildren get money up to the generation skipping tax (GST) exemption now.[16] So $2 million will go into this portion of the trust tax-free. This trust has the applicable credit provisions built into it. All of the remaining assets, less taxes and expenses, go into the previously mentioned spendthrift

[16] *See Glossary, 8.*

trusts for the children. Then, at the last child's death, the assets pass to the grandchildren."

One more question, "Are you the trustee for all the trusts?"

"Yes."

After review of the documents, everything appeared in order. I couldn't find any fault with the planning. The three children would just get income, but could not invade principal. The grandchildren would get the residue relatively tax-free. There may be some GST tax at the end, but there was no way to avoid it. I was ready to strike. He was pretty confident until my next question.

"I guess we have one trust left. Are you ready to go over the life insurance trust?" I asked Adam.

"Yes, here it is. You'll find standard provisions that I can buy assets from her estate or lend money to the estate to pay taxes. Again, after the estate is settled, the proceeds are all going into the spendthrift trust. As you can see, Arthur, the three children can't get to any of the principal, and I handle all the liquidation of the property. I think you already know we tried to buy more life insurance. Not only was it prohibitively expensive, but we also were already beyond the Crummey provision, and we were using some of her gift tax credit to pay the premium on the original policy.[17] Unfortunately, over the past few years, the premium has gone up. Alex wasn't very happy, but she knew there was nothing else she could do. She needed the life insurance."

I was devastated. I had shot a blank. Adam had recovered; he knew everything was in order. He knew he had all his bases covered. I had no more questions, and he knew it.

"Well, Arthur, unless you have additional questions, I have work to do."

What I thought was so promising had turned into a total defeat.

[17] See Glossary, 7.

As I left, he said, "Remember, Arthur, you can't disclose any of what was said today to the Sheriff unless you feel it pertains to the homicide."

"Yes."

"So before you leave, I want to be straight. Was there anything? Did everything appear in order?"

"Everything appeared in order. That's what I'm going to say to the Sheriff."

He wasn't going to let me off easily. Now I was the one who felt like I had been out on an all-night binge.

"Arthur, let this go. She died of a heart attack."

If he had just shut up, I would have left. But when he said heart attack, my brain jolted into action. Reading through all the trust documents had put me to sleep. Before I left, I tried one last time.

"Just for your information, Adam, the Sheriff and I will be revisiting Sam Waters. Sam seemed out-of-sorts about Alex's life insurance policy. The carrier probably needs to know about the possible homicide."

Even from across the room, the smell of guilt came back. Sam Waters was somehow involved, but how I didn't know. Adam knew something. There was nothing more here for me. Now I needed the Sheriff to go with me to see Sam Waters. I called the Sheriff and asked him to schedule that appointment.

CHAPTER EIGHT

Dale

Dale was waiting for me outside. Until I saw Dale, I had completely forgotten about Gibby. Dale stood, and I immediately understood why the Sheriff sent him. He was about the same height as Gibby but about 100 pounds lighter. The term "physically fit" would be perfect. Without saying anything, I motioned him outside.

"Dale, you see Gibby around?" I asked.

"No."

Gibby is too big to hide, so I knew he was gone. I doubt he can take the heat outside for very long. And Florida humidity can wilt a person. Gibby must have given up waiting for me. Despite Goldie's substantial breakfast, I was getting hungry.

"Dale, after we have some lunch, I have to find Gibby. He's next on my list," I mentioned.

Dale asked me how Gibby had looked.

"What do you mean?"

"Did he look hung over, like he spent the whole night drinking?" Dale asked.

I just nodded my head.

"Then he's at home sleeping it off," Dale said casually.

"Oh, so it's that simple?"

"Yeah, it's pretty simple when it comes to Gibby. But I think the Sheriff should go with us!"

"Ok, I guess, but you look like you can handle Gibby without the Sheriff's help."

Dale shook his head. "No," he said.

"I'll explain during lunch, but I'm going to call the Sheriff. He may even bring along another deputy. If we wake Gibby up, no telling how he will react. One thing's for certain. After this, you can't be out of my sight. Gibby isn't to be trusted."

"That bad?" I wondered.

"Worse. Most people wouldn't dare pull a gun out in broad daylight. Sounds like you're lucky to be alive after this morning," Dale said thoughtfully.

At lunch Dale explained his past friendship and present dislike for Gibby. They had grown up together. In grade school they had a great relationship. Both were exceptional athletes, but Dale was better and more popular. The local newspapers frequently reported his athletic accomplishments. To add insult to injury, Gibby's sister Dawn was interested in Dale. Gibby saw his chance to sabotage Dale towards the end of senior year football. During a practice, he blindsided Dale; Gibby went for Dale's knee. The result was that the injury was permanent. The college recruiters' phone calls stopped. With rehab, no offers of athletic scholarships, and limited family financial assistance, Dale settled for the work force. Normally, the Sheriff's department wouldn't hire Dale because his knee limited him. But since the Sheriff was an old family friend, he made an exception. After a pause, Dale went on.

"The gossip around town after the knee surgery was that Gibby was bragging about taking me out. Something happened after his dad died. He turned mean. That's why we need the Sheriff along. Gibby is going to be hard to handle. If he gets too smart with you, I'm liable to lose my temper," he said.

"Thanks."

So much for using lunch to lick my wounds. Instead, I could only look forward to being thrown into the lion's den. I'd had my share of difficult clients but never a brute like Gibby. I was glad that the Sheriff would be around not only when I saw Gibby but also when I saw Dawn. Dale, on the other hand, was both an asset and a liability to questioning Gibby and Dawn.

CHAPTER NINE

Gibby

Gibby lived on the edge of town in a relatively new but run-down house. Although the weeds had been cut down and there wasn't any litter, the house looked unkempt. Gibby's car was parked on the lawn. While Dale and I waited for the Sheriff in the car, Dale spoke freely about Gibby.

"Gibby is about my age, thirty-seven. He was a good high school football player. Maybe not all-state, but good. The university offered him an athletic scholarship mainly because Tom had been a respected player on the team and because Alex and Tom made sizable donations to the university. Gibby quickly learned that playing at the university level was a lot different from being a high school star. All the university players were stars in high school. Gibby mainly played with the second unit. His dirty play in practice was noticed not only by players but also by the coaches. Gibby thought it was funny to blindside his teammates, and his coaches' reprimands did little to deter him. He knew he wasn't going to get kicked off the team. But by his senior year, he was fat and mainly warmed the bench, even in practice," Dale explained.

"Being on the team his freshman year, in a top-notch fraternity, and a seemingly funny guy, he cut a swath through the college girls in his early years. By the end of college, he couldn't get a date because of his reputation."

Dale went on to say that no one knew if Gibby even graduated. If he did graduate, then he definitely didn't take advantage of a college education. When Gibby returned home, he never worked because his mother supported him and bought him new cars. At first, he attracted money-hungry so-called friends, but when the money ran out a few years ago, most people abandoned him. Then two land developers noticed his situation and wined and dined him. Even that ceased when the developers overbuilt Florida. Gibby has resorted to drinking cheap beer. The word around town is that he is hopelessly in debt and his mother refused to bail him out.

"Has he ever been married?" I asked.

"No."

That didn't surprise me. Just about that time the Sheriff and another deputy arrived. The Sheriff wasn't taking any chances from the look on his face. He wasn't wasting any words when he spoke.

"Arthur, considering your description of Gibby a few hours ago and given that the house is completely closed up, you need to stay away. When we wake him, he'll be pissed. Sorry, Dale, you need to stay away too. I don't trust you with Gibby," the Sheriff said.

The Sheriff and deputy then approached the house. They first rang the doorbell, but when nothing happened, they tried knocking. After no response, they pounded. Still no response. He was in the house, hibernating like a bear in winter. The Sheriff returned to his car and pulled a bullhorn out of the trunk. He walked to the window of the room where he believed Gibby was sleeping.

When he got close to the window, he yelled full force into the bullhorn, "Gibby, this is the Sheriff. You have thirty seconds to open the front door."

The bullhorn was loud enough that people down the street came out of their houses to see what was happening. The Sheriff and deputy waited at the front door. In about thirty seconds, the front door opened. It was dark inside, like a cave. The Sheriff ordered Gibby to step out. Gibby didn't budge. Once again, the Sheriff put the bullhorn to his mouth. He was relatively certain that Gibby couldn't stand another blast. He was right because Gibby came out into the bright, hot, humid day clad in a pair of athletic shorts. He was huge. The Sheriff motioned me to come over. When Gibby saw me, his temperature and temper rose.

"Sheriff, what's this jerk doing here?" he asked.

I didn't move. I decided to wait this out. He may be overweight, but I bet he was quick. I have seen a big gator move faster than a person can run for a short distance. If he can play football at the university level, he had to be quick.

The Sheriff replied, "Arthur's here to ask you some questions."

"Like hell he is. What am I charged with?"

"Assault with a deadly weapon."

"You can't prove that," Gibby said defensively.

I remained quiet and let Gibby and the Sheriff go at it. Gibby was looking directly into the sun, and I could see sweat beads forming all over his body. The heat of the sun and the humidity were my friends. With Gibby's sleep deprivation, it wouldn't be long before the elements caught up with him. The Sheriff knew what to do. If he could keep him in the sun, the Sheriff could roast this pig. When Gibby began to look cooked, the Sheriff tried again.

"Gibby, if you want to go back into the house, then you have to answer Arthur's questions. Otherwise, we'll stay out here for as long as it takes."

Gibby was swaying in the heat. He longed for the air conditioning. Finally, Gibby mumbled "OK" and went inside. The Sheriff motioned to me to follow him in. I was immediately sorry I had entered the house. It was cooler, but it smelled like an unwashed drunk, and it was a filthy mess. The Sheriff nodded at me to get started with my questions. Besides the smell, the Sheriff didn't want to be confined with Gibby in a small living room. Before anyone could draw a gun, Gibby could make a move. Gibby plopped down in a big, old chair. I wanted to get this over with as quickly as possible.

"Gibby, where were you yesterday morning?"

"What time?"

"Before the big thunderstorm hit. The morning your mother died."

"Sleeping, I guess, because I didn't know it rained."

"Where were you before that, like early morning?"

"I was at Joe's bar. I had been drinking with Adam. He paid our bar tab and left between midnight and one o'clock. Joe set me up with enough beer to last for a couple of hours. Even Joe left, and I locked up when I left. It was early dawn, and I came straight home."

"Anyone see you in the morning when you got home?"

"No."

I was watching Gibby's body language. As he talked, he had gone from being relaxed to sitting on the edge of his chair. He was waking up. He could be dangerous. I was only ten feet away. I had maybe five or ten minutes before he would explode. I looked at the Sheriff. He saw my glance and moved his hand closer to his gun. I continued.

"In front of Adam's office this morning, you accused me of your mother's death," I stated.

"You got that right, you son-of-a-bitch."

"How did you know she died of a heart attack? The Sheriff told Adam that it was a homicide, not a heart attack. There was no mention of a heart attack."

"Sheriff, do I need an attorney?"

This guy was street savvy. He could see where this line of questioning was leading. Before the Sheriff could answer, I continued my questioning. If he decided he wanted an attorney, we would have to leave. I had to press on. I didn't even look at the Sheriff.

"Gibby, what do you know about your mother's financial planning?"

"I guess I get a third of her assets after taxes. My mom and Adam didn't tell me much. I did hear my mom say that the Grove should be sold when she died."

"Is that what you plan to do if you have a choice?"

"Yeah, sell it to the highest bidder, pay the taxes, and leave town. I don't care about family ownership. The ups and downs of citrus groves in the past years aren't part of my future plans. I'm tired of asking for money."

"I understand you were friendly with a couple of land developers."

I was still keeping a wary eye on Gibby.

"They were ready to buy the Grove until home sales dropped. I even took one of them out to see my mother. He tried to pressure her until she pulled the gun out of her living room table. My mom had a temper. I inherited that. Since the building slump, the developers won't even buy me a beer."

"Do you think they'll still bid on the property?" I asked.

"Maybe stink bid or maybe not at all. The banks may not lend them the money."

This wasn't going anywhere, and Gibby knew it. I couldn't prove anything. Might as well try my only remaining card.

"You know about the life insurance policy on your mother's life?"

"Yep." No reaction, nothing. Just a blank expression.

"Do your sisters know about your mother's death?" I asked.

"Yep."

The Sheriff saw I was getting nowhere. He informed Gibby to keep away from the Grove and from me. Gibby just nodded. I left feeling uneasy. The Sheriff promised me that Dale would be with me twenty-four hours a day. He would be staying at the Grove house at night just down the hall from me. At my age, I don't want to get beat up by a brute like Gibby. I may never mend. I would never take him on even if he could hardly walk.

CHAPTER TEN

The Sheriff's Office

I got into Dale's car, and we followed the Sheriff back to his office. I needed a little time to get my thoughts together. I was glad that Dale said very little. He didn't even ask about what had happened in Gibby's house. He probably realized that we had gotten nowhere since we were in the house such a short time and left without Gibby. I just stared blankly out the window. We pulled up outside the Sheriff's office and went inside. It was mid-afternoon, and the Sheriff and I needed to plan our next course of action.

"Sheriff, I have very little for you. Both Sam and Adam act weird when the life insurance policy is mentioned. I think you should call Sam and arrange a meeting for tomorrow. Maybe your coming will worry him. I also need to talk to the two daughters. Can you arrange for us to see them tomorrow also?" I asked.

"Arthur, you look wiped out."

"I'm exhausted. This is hard work. I hope something happens this afternoon to bring this case to a conclusion. If something with the life insurance or the girls doesn't pan out, I'm going home tomorrow evening."

The Sheriff just nodded his head. We had absolutely nothing. Then he said, "Alex's death was determined to be a heart

67

attack. That means I have only one more day to keep the homicide investigation open."

"Sheriff, that seals it. It's now or never," I said.

The Sheriff just stared at me. I knew he wanted to find the killer, but we were getting nowhere. This wasn't some made-for-TV movie where someone confesses out of the blue. We had no witnesses and actually a weak motive because real estate development had gone into the tank. I needed to get back to work I could do. I wasn't trained to do homicide detective work. My thoughts shifted back to some unfinished business.

"Goldie and I can't take staying in the house much longer. If I leave, the house needs to be closed up."

The Sheriff looked concerned when I mentioned leaving without considering Goldie's needs.

"Where is Goldie going to stay?" he asked.

"Sheriff, you might not know this, but Goldie has plenty of money. She can do whatever she wants, but she can't stay in the house all alone. I'm sure she has some friends in town she can stay with temporarily," I explained.

He still looked concerned, but he nodded his head. "Arthur, I'll still ask around. Goldie and Alex had a nice life out at the Grove. It's been Goldie's home for most of her life."

Even though what he said was true, the house needed to be closed up unless something happened. Without me there, Goldie had no one to talk to, and I didn't know if she could even drive a car. Dale was also going to stay at the house tonight. Rather than both of us driving, I suggested he just ride with me. I wasn't going to go anywhere without him. I was sure Goldie would like him around.

As we rode out to the Grove, Dale looked as though he felt uneasy. He was going to stay in a house that belonged to a woman who might have been his mother-in-law, a woman who was now dead. Dale and Alex had remained friends even after he and Dawn split up. He was one of the few people who knew of the relationship between the Sheriff and Alex. For all concerned, I believed this should be the last night in the house. I planned to tell Goldie to start packing her personal belongings tomorrow.

CHAPTER ELEVEN

The Grove House

The Grove house came into view, and Goldie was sitting on the front porch in one of the old white rockers. She looked relieved to see us coming up the road late in the afternoon. She knew Dale, and the two of them had a comfortable relationship. Dale was single and had taught himself to be a good cook, so he and Goldie prepared dinner. If we decided to leave, Goldie would have to give the remaining food away.

Frankly, most of my clients are only that—clients. I don't have a personal relationship with them, and I like it that way. But I was now involved in this case on a more personal level, and I wasn't sure how I felt about that. Dale and I followed Goldie into the house and sat down with her at the kitchen table. After a short time, I decided that I would leave the two of them alone to talk about old times. They could be more relaxed without me there. The Sheriff had been right, I *was* wiped out. I went upstairs to think things out.

While they were working and talking in the kitchen, I had a plan of my own. I hadn't forgotten about the trains. I found all of the trains, tracks, transformers, little houses, and a train station. I decided to set them up in the upstairs hallway near my sleeping room. That way I didn't have to move the train layout very far, and I could try out all the locomotives. Since I knew the locomotives hadn't been used in years, I ran each of them for just a few minutes. Everything was like new. When I had everything out, I just stood and stared at it. I could see Alex with her father at Christmas. Just as I started to put everything away, Dale came up to get me for dinner. I left the track and the little houses where they were and followed Dale down.

As I sat down, I realized how hungry I was. Goldie and Dale had prepared a meal of shrimp scampi with pasta Emeril-style. I helped myself to a generous portion and was pleasantly surprised at how delicious it was. A Caesar salad and hot bread completed the meal with a bottle of Chardonnay. We lingered over dinner, talking about various dinner experiences—especially disastrous wedding receptions and banquets. We all had personal humorous stories to contribute. Each of us tried hard to keep the conversation light.

After dinner I called the Sheriff about tomorrow's activities. He still hadn't heard from Alex's daughters, who seemed to have disappeared. We did have an appointment to meet with Sam at 9:00 A.M. The Sheriff commented that Sam had very little to say when he spoke with him about a morning meeting. I suggested spending the rest of the morning with the land developer who had been the most interested in Alex's property. The Sheriff laughed and reminded me that the land developer's car was the one that Alex had shot up. The Sheriff agreed to arrange a meeting with him.

By now it was getting late. We decided to call it an early night since the open windows and doors would light the house up early the next morning with the summer sun. The breeze was scarce, and this night was hot and sticky. Somehow I managed to fall into a deep sleep.

A tremendous cry woke everyone, followed by a thud that shook the second floor. I had to force myself to wake up, and

I immediately heard Dale outside my door. At about the same time, the hallway lights went on and revealed Gibby sprawled all over the train tracks and little houses I had left out in the hallway. He was rising fast to meet Dale head on. Gibby had apparently entered the house in his bare feet. He hadn't turned on any lights since he knew the house like the back of this hand. He was gunning for me and had stepped and fallen on the little houses with their sharp metal roofs. I could see he was wounded. The train layout had saved my life.

Soon Dale and Gibby were tangled in a bar brawl. On one side of the hall the plastered wall was already broken through. Unfortunately, Gibby was a far superior fighter, especially in a tight space. I decided against jumping on Gibby as I suspected he would swat me away like a fly. When I could see that he was just about to finish Dale, I darted past Gibby to distract him. He wanted me; Dale was simply a surprise. He saw me go down the stairs about the same time I saw Goldie on the first floor. I yelled at her to get into a safe spot and to call the Sheriff. She disappeared. I was after the gun. I knew that the only way to stop Gibby was to shoot him.

As I charged into the living room, I pulled the gun out of the table drawer and checked to make sure the safety was off. I heard Gibby pounding down the stairs and barreling into the room. Without a warning, I just pulled the trigger. With one bullet he lost his right kneecap, but he kept coming. He was nearing the table when I fired the second shot, taking out his left kneecap. He collided with the heavy oak table and lay unconscious. I ran to get Dale's handcuffs. Only after Gibby's hands were cuffed behind his back did I breathe easily.

Most of my friends know I hate guns, but that doesn't mean I can't shoot. In fact, I'm a crack shot. I didn't want to kill Gibby. I just wanted to solve the murder, and I knew I couldn't do that without him. Knowing that both Gibby and

Dale needed medical attention, I knocked on Goldie's locked door.

"Goldie, did you get the Sheriff?" I asked.

The fear in Goldie's voice was palpable.

"Arthur, I tried and tried, but the phone is always busy."

Although I was worried about Goldie's well-being, I couldn't hide my irritation. Why would the phone at the Sheriff's office be constantly busy?

"Goldie, this doesn't make any sense. It's two o'clock in the morning. Keep trying. Also try EMS. Gibby lost two kneecaps and can't move. I'm going upstairs to see about Dale."

Dale lay in the hallway. I wiped his face with a wet towel. He writhed in pain, holding his ribs and knee. Wow, all of that in a matter of minutes. I wouldn't have had a chance against Gibby. I let Dale know that we couldn't get through to the Sheriff's office but that Goldie was calling EMS. He seemed relieved. Through clenched teeth, Dale asked about Gibby. He responded with a satisfied smile when I told him that Gibby would need two knee replacements. Since he seemed stable, I hurried back downstairs.

"Goldie, any luck?"

"No, all the lines are busy. I don't understand why," she said.

I tried to remain calm, but I was becoming increasingly annoyed and frightened.

"Keep trying," I instructed.

I knew that what I was about to do wasn't fair play. However, I wasn't going to miss an opportunity to obtain some much needed information. Gibby was coming around. I was glad I had him cuffed. He had a deep gash across his forehead, and I knew that as soon as he came to, the pain in his knees would hit him. I sat patiently across the room. Finally, when the pain hit his senses, I had his attention. I was sure he would hate me forever, but I didn't care. He let out a grunt, a growl, and a string of profanity. When he tried to roll over toward where I was sitting to face me, the pain hit him hard. I knew that I had to take advantage of his agony.

"Gibby, now listen to me. If you move, the pain will get worse. We can't reach anyone in town, so EMS isn't going to be here anytime soon. There aren't any painkillers in the house, but there are bottles of liquor. Do you want a drink?"

He mumbled more profanity but with less intensity. Which was a good sign.

"Listen, Gibby, I have all night to wait you out. I'm going to get myself something to drink and bring a bottle for you. If you cooperate, I'll share the liquor," I said. "You think about it."

When I came back, he quickly but quietly agreed to cooperate. I rolled him on his side so I wouldn't drown him and gave him a big chug of whiskey. I didn't waste any time.

"Ok, I need to know about your mother."

Gibby was forthcoming with his answers.

"I didn't kill her," Gibby said. "Fact is, I hadn't seen her in two or three days before she died."

"What happened when you saw her?"

"I asked her for money. The local bank is on my back."

"For your house loan?"

Gibby seemed to be loosening up. The whiskey was working.

"Naw, I signed a personal note. The bank thought I owned a portion of the Grove. With all the problems now with sub-prime loans, the bank wants its money."

"How much?"

"A million dollars."

"Why did you need a million dollars?" I wondered.

"Roger Stallings wanted us to get into a new development he was buying."

"Who is Roger Stallings, and who is us?"

"Me and my mom's attorney, Adam. I needed to make some money. My mother was tough. When she cut me off, I had to do something. I knew she wasn't going to change her mind. I didn't kill her. I actually admired her fortitude."

"Do you know who killed her?"

"No, and if I did, I probably would kill them, even my own worthless sisters. Mom mentioned that they both had been by begging for money. Mom was fed up with money issues. She got so upset she had to take a nitro tablet."

"Ok, back to Adam. How is he involved?" I queried.

"Well, both of us believed Mom would live for years. Adam was handling all these lucrative land deals for stupid locals. He believed we could make a killing with Roger."

"How much did he put into the pot?"

"More than I did but he got a big inheritance when his daddy died."

Gibby was cooperating. I believed he was telling the truth. I gave him another big chug of liquor to keep him talking.

"Gibby, what do you know about your mother's life insurance?"

"All I know is that I have to sign off each year on the money that's put into the trust to pay the life insurance premium."

"That's it?"

"Yep. I need more than one swallow. Give me enough to kill the pain and knock me out."

I let him have a long series of chugs, and he looked pretty much out of it. I really didn't know what else to ask him. I still felt the life insurance had something to do with Alex's death.

But what? Gibby had just explained the typical Crummey gift provision of the irrevocable life insurance trust.[18]

Just then Goldie told me that EMS was on the way. I asked her to go upstairs to see how Dale was doing and to stay with him. She glared at me when she saw Gibby. The look in her eyes spoke volumes. She had raised Gibby. She loved him, and he looked awful. He had wet his pants, and it was painful for her to see him like this. I didn't know if she could forgive me. Maybe Alex did simply die from a heart attack. I sensed that I might have gone too far. I should have turned the Sheriff down and gone home. Too late now. I was in too deep and needed to solve this mystery.

[18] See Glossary, 7 and 10.

CHAPTER TWELVE

Death Revisited

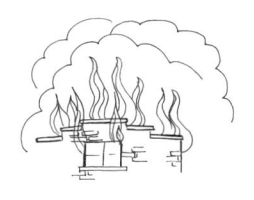

After EMS left with Dale and Gibby, I sat alone in the house. Goldie had accompanied them to the hospital, and the house was eerily quiet. So far I really didn't have a definite explanation for Alex's death. Suddenly, the silence was shattered by the ringing of the telephone. It was the Sheriff.

"You ok?" he asked.

"I'm ok, but Dale is banged up. Goldie is with Dale and Gibby at the hospital."

I told him about the shooting, what Gibby had said, and finally how Goldie looked at me. Then the Sheriff explained why his phones had been tied up.

"Arthur, someone torched the insurance agency and possibly Sam. We can't tell for certain; the body was burned to a crisp. Hopefully, the teeth will reveal the identity of the victim. The fire was so bad it destroyed three other buildings in town. That's why you couldn't get through to my office or EMS. Our fire department couldn't contain the fire, and two firemen are badly burned. There is no question that this is arson to cover up murder.

"Any idea who did it?" I asked.

"No, no idea. I'm not even sure that the body is Sam."

"What time did the fire start?"

"Around midnight," he replied.

"Gibby came into the house before 2:00 A.M. I had no idea what was going on. Too bad I didn't know about the fire. I had him on the ropes with questions, but I have a feeling he wasn't involved."

"You know, Arthur, your question to Sam about crop insurance must have hit home because he came over to talk to me about threats from grove owners," the Sheriff replied.

"You think one of them would do it?"

"It's pretty extreme," he said, considering the thought.

"I suppose his office is burned to the ground."

"Yeah, nothing left."

"Sheriff, I'm not going to be any good until I get some sleep. Who are we scheduled to see tomorrow? I guess I should say today."

"Well, Roger the land developer is coming around 11:00 A.M., and we're still chasing down Alex's two daughters. We have the drug-buying locations around the area under constant surveillance. Dawn will show up."

"Okay, I'll call you around 9:00 A.M. I'm going to try to get some shut-eye," I said.

My gut feeling was that Sam's death was somehow connected to Alex's death. Someone wanted to shut up Sam and destroy all the insurance records. It could be related to the crop insurance, but I doubted it was. I hung up the phone, and the house became still. I sat in the overstuffed chair in Alex's father's room. I dozed off. Maybe the spirit of Alex would tell me something while I slept.

Around dawn I awoke. The windows were still open, and a fresh breeze agitated the curtains. I decided to walk around the Grove. My head was pounding, and nothing made sense. How could I have caused two deaths in two days? I was sure it had something to do with money. But what?

After a light breakfast, I called the Sheriff's office. He wasn't in yet. I decided to inventory the trains and put them away. Some of the houses were squashed. Some pointed parts had blood on them. These little mangled pieces of metal were my friends. I wondered what would happen to them. Goldie called me from the hospital to tell me that she couldn't come back to the house. She wanted to be with Gibby. She explained that she would stay at the hospital for now. She gave me instructions for locking up the house and promised to call the Sheriff's office with any news. The Sheriff called me shortly thereafter. They had caught Dawn, and she was in jail. She was in bad shape and needed to be hospitalized. He knew he could only keep her for a few hours at most.

"Arthur, I need you here right away."

"Ok, I'm leaving now."

The Sheriff and I decided that he would do the questioning since Dawn knew him well and would probably be more receptive to him. The Sheriff knew that as soon as the rehab people were involved, it might be a month or so before he could talk to her again.

As soon as I saw her, I knew he was right. She was skin and bones. She was likely high and was trying to look calm, but as soon as the drugs wore off, anything might happen. The Sheriff started right in.

"Dawn, I need to ask you some questions."

"I didn't do anything wrong! You can't prove anything!" she exclaimed.

She couldn't sit still. She was squirming in her chair and kept picking at her skin. She was having a hard time concentrating. The Sheriff knew he had to ask simple questions.

"Dawn, where were you on the morning of your mother's death?"

"I don't know."

"What?"

"I don't know one day from another," she said.

Somehow I believed her. She was cooperative. She wasn't fighting the Sheriff. He continued on.

"Ok, who were you with over the past few days?"

"I stay with a bunch of people."

"Can any of them verify where you were?" the Sheriff asked.

"I don't know."

This was going nowhere, and the Sheriff could sense it. He skillfully shifted to a more direct question.

"Dawn, when was the last time you saw your mother?"

It took her a few minutes to respond.

"I think it was three or four days ago. I went out to the house in the morning."

"What happened?"

Her eyes rolled. She looked like she almost passed out. Then, she blurted out, "She greeted me by saying, 'Look what the cat dragged in.' My mother and I don't get along and haven't for years."

"Why did you go there?"

"I needed money. I owe some people in town big time. Because they know I'm Alex's daughter, they let me run up a tab," she said. "That morning they wouldn't give me any more drugs until I paid them in full."

"Did she give you any money?"

"No, she wanted to commit me to rehab. She threatened to call you. Before she could call you, I left."

I couldn't resist; I had to ask more questions.

"Dawn, was Goldie around when you were at the house?"

"No, I didn't see or hear her."

It sure sounded like Dawn was actually at the house the morning Alex died. It had to be sometime after Goldie and I went to town. I had to make sure.

"Had it rained yet?"

"No, about the time we got back to town, the rain started."

"Who is 'we'? Who was with you?"

"Lefty."

"Dawn, how do you feel about your mother's death?"

"I can't say I'm sorry. I could never live up to her expectations. Gibby will sell the Grove, and with him in control, I won't have to beg for money. When I left the house, Mom was just about ready to blow up."

"Did she go for her gun?"

"No, Lefty knew about the gun incident, so he kept the motor running. When I came out, we left."

"Where were you last night during the fire?"

"I don't know."

I was relatively sure that Dawn had not killed Alex. It had to be someone who came after her. She merely had caused Alex to lose her cool and was guilty only of destroying the morning's calm. Dawn started to rant and rave. Whatever she had taken was starting to wear off.

"My mother was a witch. When my father died, everything changed. All my mother cared about was the Grove. She dumped us. When I started using drugs, she knew it and ignored it. I'm glad she died. I'm going to spend every cent I can get on drugs."

She continued ranting and raving, moving constantly around the room. The Sheriff looked concerned. He got up to constrain her just as she bashed her head against the wall. She was ok, but the Sheriff stopped the interview. He left with her. I sat, stunned by what I had just witnessed. Generally, I deal with older clients. For the most part, I only have to deal with alcohol problems. The drug problems are usually associated with my client's children and grandchildren, and I stay out of that.

When the Sheriff returned, he looked drained. I could see Dawn in his eyes—much the same way that Gibby affected Goldie. I knew he would do everything he could to save Dawn. However, I agreed with what he said.

"Arthur, she didn't do it." She's so frail that she couldn't hurt a mouse. I'll check Lefty out, but he's also a 90-pound weakling. If something had been stolen out of the house, they would be my suspects, but Goldie said nothing was missing."

"Sheriff, I must leave today. I can't spend another night in the house."

"Arthur, I realize that. Let's take an inventory of who is out and who is in."

I thought that was a strange way to put it.

"Sheriff, I think Gibby and Dawn are out. Sam was out because I was with him. We have one daughter, a couple of advisors, and maybe two land developers left. Something better pop."

CHAPTER THIRTEEN

Roger Stallings

I sat quietly in the interview room waiting for Roger Stallings, the land developer. What had started as an interesting financial planning case was turning into a pure money case. Land development in the Orlando area had been unbelievable, but the bloom of the Florida flower had faded. Roger had been interested in the Grove, and somehow Gibby had become involved with him on another project. I wondered if the two were tied together.

Before Roger arrived, the Sheriff returned. He looked exhausted. Alex, the fire, and now Dawn had robbed him of his spirit. I hoped he'd allow me to take the lead with Roger.

"Sheriff, let me handle Roger. I started this mess; let me finish it."

He grunted in reply. But I had found my second wind. I was primed. Maybe I could make it to the finish line. Roger arrived dressed in an outfit accented with an abundance of ostentatious gold jewelry. He greeted the office staff loudly with attention-getting fanfare. He obviously didn't understand that this was not a morning to be boisterous in the Sheriff's office. The Sheriff stormed out of his private office.

"Roger, get your ass in the interview room."

I was already in the interview room, and I heard the Sheriff's command to Roger. Roger let out a high-pitched "squeak" when he opened the door and saw me.

"Who are you?" Roger squeaked.

"My name is Arthur, and I'm going to interview you."

"Like hell you are. Not without my attorney."

Just about that time, the Sheriff came in. He had obviously heard Roger's comment to me because he leaned down almost nose-to-nose with Roger. Neither man looked very happy.

"Okay, Roger, but until your attorney shows up, I'm going to put you in a cell with two sex offenders. They don't like each other, but they will like you," the Sheriff said.

The Sheriff flung open the door and called for a deputy.

"Sheriff, hold on," Roger said panicking.

"Do you or don't you want an attorney?"

"It depends on what you're charging me with."

"Nothing, right now. Arthur needs to ask you some questions. If you feel uncomfortable with the questioning, you can ask for an attorney. But for right now, just answer the questions."

Roger relaxed slightly, his defenses weakening.

"Okay, Sheriff, but I reserve the right to ask for an attorney," Roger said.

I began my questioning.

"Roger, when was the last time you saw Alex?"

Roger answered without hesitation. He seemed especially anxious to talk about Alex shooting his car.

"The day she shot up my car. Sometime after that I found another property to buy, and then the housing market turned."

I needed to know definitively that Roger wasn't interested in the Grove.

"So you're not interested in the Grove?" I asked.

"No, it's too big a property."

I knew I was pushing my luck, but I took my chances.

"Gibby says he invested a million dollars with you," I said.

"Yes."

"Is this the new property you recently bought?"

"Yes."

"Tell me about the property."

At mention of the property, he became boastful; I let him talk.

"I've seen the rise and fall of Florida real estate. The 1973-75 bust is still fresh in my mind. I figured we were due for another bust. I sold all my developed land and houses and bought the new property. As soon as I bought it, I announced that I was going to sell shares. I would be the general partner, and I would sell limited partnership interests.

He continued, "Anyhow, the word got around, and I sold the limited partnership interests for three times what I bought the property for. The extra money was supposed to be for marketing and land improvement. When the market turned soft, I didn't do anything. The money is sitting in an interest bearing account. All the limited partnership owners can verify that the money is there. This is a clean deal."

"So you are still getting salary as a general partner?"

"Yeah, it's a sweet deal for me," Roger said.

"So how do the limited partners feel?"

"Most of them were Johnny-come-latelies. The boom always catches them at the end when the rainbow is about to evaporate. When they came running with their money, I knew it was time to get my money out."

"Is this when Gibby and Adam showed up?" I continued.

"Yep. They wanted in. They were afraid I would sell all the units before they could raise their money. Gibby promised that when Alex died, he would keep me in mind for the Grove property. That was good enough for me to let them have some time."

"I know Gibby got a loan from a bank. What happened with Adam?"

"Well, Gibby tried to get the money from his mother, but she turned him down. Adam convinced the bank that Gibby had an ownership interest in the Grove. That's how Gibby got his money."

I repeated my question. I needed to know about Adam's involvement.

"What about Adam?"

"I don't know much except that the bank made him a loan also."

"How much did he put in?"

Roger's demeanor immediately changed. His shoulders stiffened, and his jaw tightened. He was obviously guarded in his response.

"To get that information you will have to subpoena the partnership. Adam is an attorney, and I don't want to be sued."

"Ok, Gibby told me that he and Adam both invested. Did Adam invest more than Gibby?" I asked.

A deep, hoarse grunt escaped Roger's throat.

"How do the limited partners feel about their investment?" I queried.

"They want their money back. Many of them acquired bank loans to invest, and now the banks are calling in the loans."

"Like Gibby and probably Adam."

"Yep, both Gibby and Adam have been after me to buy their limited partnership interest back. Gibby and Adam were pressuring me. It went so far that Adam told me that he would control the Grove property sale when Alex died. I told them I could buy the interest back at 50 cents on a dollar at most. They were angry, but I said I would also have to buy all the other interests back at the same rate. I know the real estate downturn will pass, and I want to develop the property. It is free of debt, and I'm sitting on all the extra invested cash to pay myself and the property tax, insurance, and other expenses until the market turns."

"What happened when you made them the offer?"

"They looked sick. When they came in, I made sure that some of my construction guys were in the office with me. Gibby can lose his temper and kill you with a swat of his arm."

So did he get violent?" I asked.

"No, strangely, he said he would just file for bankruptcy. He said he was broke. It was Adam who was traumatized, especially when Gibby didn't seem concerned."

"Did Gibby or Adam come back?"

"Adam did repeatedly," Roger said.

"Did you change your offer?"

"No, in fact I dropped the offer to forty cents on a dollar."

"Where were you last night?" I asked.

"Ok, I can see where you're going. I know someone died in the fire, but I'll answer your question. I was at home with my wife. In regards to Alex, I have had my disagreements with people. Alex scared me the most when she shot up my car and the Sheriff didn't do anything about it. There is no way I would ever go out to that house again."

After Roger left, I told the Sheriff that unless something came up with Cindy, I needed to see Adam again. The Sheriff left me in the interview room. Adam was deeply involved in this case, but how was the life insurance involved? The Sheriff came back to inform me that Cindy would be in after lunch.

CHAPTER FOURTEEN

Insurance

Since the insurance files were destroyed and Adam had already shown me the original life insurance contract, there was nothing else to review. It was time to ask for a favor. Some of the officers of the insurance company that covered Alex were acquaintances of mine. Through the years, a few of their big producers had been in trouble with clients and state agencies. I had either worked out settlements or won cases for them as an expert witness. Although I had been paid well, the company gained equally by keeping the big producers happy. Now I needed almost immediate help. First, I had to get someone on the phone.

I had a friend at the company named Sally who worked in the executive suite. Her son was one of those big producers I had saved. She would know who was in. There was no time for small talk. I picked up the phone and dialed her number.

"Sally, this is Arthur. I need some help."

"Hi, Arthur. How can I help you?" she asked.

"Which of the top officers are in, and what are the chances I might talk to him?"

"Why?" she asked.

"I can't tell you."

"Maybe someday over lunch?" she replied.

88

"You get me to the right person and maybe someday over dinner!"

I didn't care who I talked to. All I wanted was to talk to someone in the policy service department who could review the original application and documents. Only a high-ranking officer could pull this off. A Mr. Touhy came on the line.

"Mr. Touhy, this is Arthur. You remember me?"

"Yes, you're the expert witness on the big cases," he said.

"Mr. Touhy, I need a favor."

"Well, go ahead. Let's see if I can help you out."

"I am involved with a $5 million death claim on one of your clients."

"Did the agent make a mistake?" he asked.

Mr. Touhy's voice was anxious. I decided to take advantage of his apprehension. My answer was critical. There was nothing wrong with the policy that I could see, so I lied.

"Possibly. The agent was a general lines broker who didn't know a lot about life insurance owned by a trust."

Not trying to conceal his irritation, Mr. Touhy responded.

"Shit, we should never let the marketing department allow brokers to sell our policies."[19]

This company had been agent-oriented for years. Only agents of the company could sell the policies. About ten years ago they opened their door to independent agents or brokers.

"I can possibly clean this whole unfortunate issue up if I can have someone pull the application file and talk to me over the phone," I said.

"Well, I don't know."

His reluctance was expected. I was asking for a lot.

"I don't need to see the file, just talk about it."

"Well, I don't know."

---

[19] See Glossary, 4.

"Mr. Touhy, this involves a double homicide, and a beneficiary may be the murderer. Your company could get a lot of bad press because the broker may be involved."

At this point, truth was not an issue with me. At least part of what I said was true.

"I can't make this decision alone," he said.

Mr. Touhy still wasn't budging. My threats weren't enough to sway him.

"I understand, but if you agree, I need to talk to someone today, preferably in an hour or two."

"What?"

"Someday one of your big producers is going to get into trouble. You know it, and I know it. I will not only take on the defense for free, but I also promise you twice my normal effort. By the way, this $5 million case won't cost you anything," I remarked.

I was willing to promise anything to get to that file. So far the trip was a financial disaster for me. Now I was agreeing to work for free! This was certainly not what I expected when I agreed to do a favor for Harry!

"Mr. Touhy, can I call you in an hour?"

I knew I wasn't going to get answers or assistance from him until he had time to process my request.

"Give me two hours."

"Ok."

I hung up the phone and found the Sheriff. I asked him if someone could get me something to eat.

"Sheriff, I pulled some strings. Hopefully, in two hours I can review the life insurance file. If there's nothing there, I'm finished. To keep Adam on edge, however, make an appointment as late as possible today. I don't care what you have to do. I have a feeling I need that appointment with Adam to wrap this up."

I needed nourishment to keep me going. I would eat whatever food was brought. The Sheriff was still busy with the fire-homicide. I couldn't help thinking that if Sam died in the fire, then the insurance information was even more important. I had just eaten the last bite of greasy fried chicken when the Sheriff popped his head in the door. He had decided to interview Cindy in his private office. I could tell by the look in his eye that this interview would be quite different from Dawn's ranting and raving.

CHAPTER FIFTEEN

Cindy

Cindy was in the Sheriff's office when I walked in. The Sheriff quickly introduced us although Cindy knew who I was. Gibby had alerted her.

Cindy had her mother's good looks, but she had tried to improve them. Her high cheekbones didn't look real. Actually, not much of her body did. The high cheekbones looked like they were added to make her look more sophisticated, but instead they removed the softness of her natural face. The features of her face didn't fit with each other. She looked like the result of plastic surgery gone wrong.

"Sheriff, why am I here? What's Arthur got to do with this?"

"I'm investigating your mother's death," the Sheriff replied.

"Why?"

"Someone may have caused her death."

Without hesitation or an ounce of compassion, she blurted out, "If they did, she deserved it."

That jolted the Sheriff. He loved Alex, and Cindy knew it. But she didn't care. The Sheriff quickly changed his line of questioning. He knew better than to show his feelings in front of Cindy.

"When did you see your mother last?" he asked.

"Three or four days ago. I saw Dawn leaving with her druggie friend."

"Why did you go to see her?"

"I needed more money to pay for my final surgical procedure. The doctors think it will take one more adjustment for everything to fit together."

"You were always pretty."

"I need to be beautiful. Pretty was ok when I was young."

"How much did you ask your mother for?"

"Thirty thousand."

The Sheriff didn't attempt to hide his amazement.

"Whew."

"I'm not using any local nip and tuck jerks. I'm using an L.A. specialist to the stars."

"What did your mother say?"

"Well, I could see that I had arrived at the wrong time, but I couldn't wait. I didn't care. I needed the money then. She told me to get lost. I threatened to cut her off from her grandchildren. I told her that I would move to L.A. with them and get involved in porno movies. I said what I thought I needed to say to get the money."

"So did you get any money?" asked the Sheriff.

"Hell, no! It got so bad she had to take one of her pills. She just sat there silently. I told her again that I would take the kids to the West Coast if I had to. Then, I left."

"So where are the children?"

"Where they normally are."

"Where is that?"

"With my ex-husband. If I go to L.A., it will be alone. I've got better things to do than raise those brats. They actually like going out to the Grove, staying in that old beat-up house, and working around the trees."

The Sheriff was visibly angry. I didn't really trust him to hold it together, and I don't think he trusted himself. He was about to lose it again. This questioning needed to end soon.

"Cindy, I have a question. Was Goldie around?" I asked.

"No."

"Was your mother alive when you left?"

"Yes, but she looked like she was ready to explode, and I couldn't care less."

"Did you see anyone drive up when you left?" I asked.

"No, I went out the front way to US-27. I wanted to get away before the storm came. Listen, all I want is my money. How soon is that going to happen?"

The Sheriff spoke up, anger in his voice, "Cindy, if I have my way, this estate won't settle until you are old and gray. I will pray to God that every procedure that you went through fails or sags. I can only hope that you become the joke of this community."

"Sheriff, I'm sorry...I..."

Cindy's lame apology was cut short by the Sheriff, "I better not see you at the funeral. You stay around town until I tell you differently. Do you understand?"

"Yes."

After she left, the Sheriff and I discussed what must have happened that morning. Alex was fine when I left. Then Dawn and Cindy came with money on their minds. Alex was still alive when Cindy left. The gun hadn't been touched. There were no tire tracks near the house when Goldie and I returned from town. The Sheriff and I agreed that whoever murdered Alex must have come and gone before the storm. The Sheriff left again to check on the second body and Adam's appointment. It was time for me to do my dirty work.

CHAPTER SIXTEEN

Life Insurance

I always talk about having grit. By that I mean persistence, energy, and the perseverance to get the job done. It was do or die on the life insurance issue. I called Mr. Touhy. Without saying much, he transferred me to Stafford who was up the chain of command. Stafford and I go way back to when I used to sell a lot of life insurance.

"Arthur, what's this all about?" Stafford asked.

"Well, one of your brokers sold my client a $5 million policy. She died suspiciously...a possible homicide. Now the broker has been killed in a possible cover-up."

I lied. I didn't know if Sam had died.

"So why do you want to review her file?"

"There is something about the life insurance policy that makes two people sweat. Sam, the insurance agent, was one of them, and now he's dead. That leaves Adam, the attorney for the insured who died," I explained.

"What do you need?" Stafford asked.

"I need an underwriter and policyholder service person to go through every piece of paper or computer file you have related to the policy with me over the phone."

"When?" he asked.

"Now. I have to meet with the client's attorney this afternoon."

This seemed to pique Stafford's interest.

"Do you think he's involved?"

"Possibly. He has the policy," I said.

"Did you see it?"

"Yes, it looks ok," I stressed, "but it may be that the ownership or beneficiary has been changed."

"Phew, I don't know. We're getting into privacy areas."

I tried to hide my irritation and urgency. I was running out of time, and I had to know what was in the documents.

"My client died. It's her policy I am talking about. I represent her."

"Arthur, this will all come out when a claim is made."

I knew he was right. If Stafford wouldn't let me review the file, no one would. I was silent.

"Arthur, how much of the underwriting and policy did you see?"

"At the agent's office I saw copies of the original application; the policy included some basic medical information and, of course, the ownership and beneficiary information. The actual policy included the same paperwork at the attorney's office."

"I can arrange to confirm the current ownership and beneficiary."

There is a time to be silent, and this was it. Something was up. I didn't say a word. He couldn't even hear me breathe.

Finally, he said, "Arthur, are you there?"

"Stafford, I don't need your help to find out the current ownership and beneficiary information. I can do that on my own."

"How?" Doubt had crept into his voice.

"I know the ownership and FID number of the trust. I only need to call into policyholder services with that information to confirm the ownership, beneficiary, cash value, and any loans. Do I need to go on? But I believe this policy is clean. I'm looking for a second policy."

"Well, we did underwrite a second policy a few years ago."

"I know that. Did you issue a policy?" I queried.

"No, we finally decided to decline. I suspect her medical information had deteriorated. I can't answer beyond that."

"How much was the application for?"

"Ten million. Arthur, I can tell you the broker went out to six or eight companies to try to obtain coverage."

"Do you know if any of them issued a policy?"

"No, but we did get an inquiry from one company to verify that our $5 million dollar policy was in force."

"Can you tell me the name of the carrier?"

He told me the carrier's name. His dismissive tone told me that our conversation was over. He couldn't help me further. At this point I had the trust federal information number from the CPA. I tried investigating the second policy by looking at the carrier's website. Without any policy number, I didn't get far. A direct telephone inquiry wouldn't work. Unfortunately, I had never sold any policies for this carrier, nor did they ever use me for expert witness work.

I called my office to do a search of my contacts file to see if the carrier's name would come up. I needed the name of someone associated with the carrier. One name came up: Bob Haverty. I wasn't sure if he would even remember me, but I had to give it a try. I was running out of time. I was lucky. He was in and took my call.

"Arthur, how are you?" Bob sounded surprised to hear from me.

After some pleasantries, I cut to the chase.

"I'm involved in a double homicide case where my client and her insurance agent have been killed."

"Are you kidding me?"

"No, and I need to find out if a life insurance policy was issued by your carrier."

"Why?" asked Bob.

"Because it may be the reason for the two deaths."

"Well, I don't know how much help I can be. Do you have a policy number?"

"No, if I had that, I wouldn't need you."

Bob sighed. "I could get into a lot of trouble."

"I have the insured's name and Social Security number, but I know the ownership isn't in her name. The policy could be owned by her trust, but I doubt that."

"I don't know." The tone of Bob's voice told me I had pushed him as hard as I should.

"This would be a big favor for me. All I need to know is whether there is a policy in force on her life. Nothing beyond that."

"When do you need it?"

"Now," I said hesitantly.

"I'll make one try with someone I know at the corporate office. Arthur, you're stretching our friendship. Where can I call you?"

While I waited, I reviewed my ethics. Was I acting as a financial planner or police officer? Since Alex died and the Sheriff hired me to investigate her death, I was really acting as a police officer. My strategies to obtain information bordered on using my financial planning knowledge. I really didn't feel satisfied with my ethics analysis. Bob's call came through. It was one word and a click.

"Yes."

I felt horrible. This was worse than trying to defend financial advisors who actually did something wrong. I just sat there. My thoughts were interrupted by the Sheriff's arrival. He confirmed it was Sam who had died. He also told me that he was under pressure to proceed on Sam's homicide investigation and drop anything to do with Alex. The coroner's report identified Alex's cause of death as a heart attack. The body had been released to the funeral home. She was scheduled to be cremated.

"Sheriff, that body's got to stay at the coroner's office. Don't let them release the body until I say so."

"Why? Do you think Adam killed her?"

"Not intentionally. But," I emphasized, "he may have caused her death."

"Why?"

"There's a second policy in force, and I think Adam owns it."

"Can you prove that?"

"No, not at this point. But I'm going to use my knowledge of the second policy with Adam. Sheriff, what's the possibility of proving Adam killed Sam?"

The Sheriff shrugged his shoulders.

"All I know is that according to the coroner, Sam died in the fire. Adam doesn't seem to have a motive for killing Sam. But there are grove owners who are still angry that Sam didn't propose that they buy crop insurance. You know how people are...always blaming the next guy for their own mistakes. Any one of them could have killed Sam."

"Did Sam give you any of the grove owners' names?"

"No."

"Now all the files are gone. Did he have any off-site computer backup?"

"I don't know about that. Maybe."

"Let's go see Adam."

CHAPTER SEVENTEEN

Adam

We arrived at Adam's office late in the afternoon—only two cars remained. Everyone was gone except the receptionist, and she left after showing us into Adam's office. The building was eerily quiet. Adam sat behind his desk. When I was here before, he didn't greet me or shake my hand. Adam was at least consistent. He was working on a file, and it took a minute or two before he looked up at the Sheriff and me. Although he didn't invite us to, we sat in the chairs across from his desk.

"What do you want?" he asked. "I have nothing else to say. Two of my friends are dead."

Interesting. Only the Sheriff knew the person killed in the fire was Sam. The Sheriff caught it right away. Out of the corner of my eye, I could see the Sheriff make a slight hand gesture toward me. I could sense he didn't want me to say anything more. I ignored him.

"How do you know it was Sam who died in the fire?" I asked.

Adam looked like he knew he had made a mistake and quickly blurted out, "I just assumed it was Sam."

"Where were you last night?" asked the Sheriff.

"I can see where you're going with this, but I didn't start the fire, and I didn't kill Sam."

I wanted Adam to feel pressured in hopes that he'd make another mistake.

"How do you know Sam was murdered? Maybe he committed suicide."

Adam could see he was getting himself in trouble.

"Arthur, I was home sleeping off a bad drunk. Gibby and I had been drinking. When he left, I went home."

Apparently, the Sheriff had decided to let me question Adam.

"What time was that?" I asked.

"About midnight."

"That's early for Gibby." I knew that Gibby would just be getting started at that hour.

"Yeah, but he said he had something to do."

"Did he say what?"

"No, but he was mad about what you and the Sheriff had done to him. He was drinking hard stuff, not beer. That makes him meaner."

"So you went home."

"Yep."

"Was Sam with you?"

"No."

"Did you go by Sam's office or home?"

"No."

I could see I was getting nowhere. The Sheriff and I had no proof that Adam was guilty. And we had no motive at this point.

"If you're finished, I need to go home."

I knew this was my last shot. I had to press on with my questions.

"You're not leaving just yet, Adam. Not until I finish."

"I'm not going to answer any more questions from you, Arthur."

The Sheriff stood up.

"Yes, you are. He works for me," he said.

"Well, make it quick. I can't see what else you could ask about Alex's death."

As I leaned toward Adam, I put my hands on the edge of his desk.

"The Sheriff and I think Alex's death and Sam's death are related."

"What?"

"Adam, there's a second policy on Alex."

"What?"

"There was a second policy issued when you tried to get her some additional coverage a few years ago. The policy is for $10 million. Where is the policy?"

"I don't know what you are talking about."

I took a deep breath and decided to go for it. I could lie with the best of them when I had to. My story wouldn't be accurate, but it would get close.

"Apparently one of the carriers agreed to issue a $10 million dollar policy. All the other carriers declined or had high premiums. You never told Alex about it. Since Sam had access to the medical records, you knew her health had gone downhill after the first policy was issued."

"The application, along with the applications with the other carriers, was signed by her as the insured, and you signed for the trust. Sam asked the carrier to issue the policy, and you put it in force with your own money. Carriers don't care where the money comes from."

Adam shifted nervously.

"You can't prove any of this," he said.

"Well, the policy is in force, and you are the owner-beneficiary. The policy was paid for with commissions Sam received and paid to you for legal fees. Sam made his quota with the company with the big commission dollars on the policy, and you washed the money through your practice."

"Arthur, you're wrong. Yes, a policy was issued, but then Alex changed her mind. She said she didn't want to get straddled with that premium."

I wasn't going to accept his answer. Since he was responding to my questions, I was determined to continue.

"Adam, she only knew that all the carriers had either declined or the premiums were excessive. She never paid any premium to put the policy in force or even knew the premium was reasonable. The money trail will show up from Sam's account to yours and will prove that you paid the premium."

"So what? She gifted me the policy."[20]

"She couldn't have gifted something she didn't own."[21]

Adam looked surprised.

"What do you mean by that?"

"The trust owns the policy, and you are the trustee."

"Ok, the trust gifted me the policy."

I was squeezing Adam in a legal vise. He didn't know insurance law the way I did.

"No, you transferred ownership and then made yourself the beneficiary after the policy was issued and paid for."

Strange as this may seem, at the time of issue there must be an insurable interest. The trust was designed to pay estate taxes at the time of Alex's death. That was the insurable interest at the time of issue. All the paperwork was correct at the time of application. After issue, the policy can be transferred to anyone as there is no insurable interest requirement. All the owner needs to do is to submit the paperwork. Adam as trustee could legally transfer the policy to himself as owner.

"I told you already. Alex didn't want the policy."

"So you transferred it to yourself."

[20] *See Glossary, 9.*
[21] *See Glossary, 14.*

"Yes, I guess you know this already."

I didn't, but he had confirmed everything so far. I figured I might as well continue.

"You made a mistake," I said.

"How? I paid all the premiums even though Sam rebated all his first year premiums."

"Adam, do you understand the principle of transfer-for-value?"[22]

"No, can't say I do."

"Well, the $10 million death benefit will be subject to ordinary income tax above any premiums paid. Uncle Sam will get $3 million or so. I doubt you've paid $1 million yet."

Adam was stunned.

"No way. Life insurance is tax free. It never was included in her estate."

My killer instinct kicked in. I went on.

"You are right about estate taxes but wrong about income taxes. I'm reporting it to the carrier. They will report it to the IRS."

"You bastard."

"In addition, since you got involved in that land deal with Roger Stallings, money must be tight. You paid the minimum premium for years. With the low interest rates paid by universal life insurance policies, the premium due is currently causing you a financial hardship."

Adam was silent. I decided to go for broke. My instincts had served me well so far.

"Adam, you caused Alex's death. You were there when she died."

"You have no proof of that."

"Sorry, Adam, we do. You saw Cindy's car and waited until she left. When she drove towards US-27, you felt safe. But she turned around a few miles down the road. She needed that

[22] See Glossary, 22.

money, so she went back. When she saw your car, she chickened out and left."

What I had just said was a total lie, but Adam didn't know that. The Sheriff twitched but kept silent. I had warned him I would lie.

"We don't know what happened in the house, but we do know that both Dawn and Cindy had driven Alex to the edge. You hit her with some kind of money issue. It could have been Gibby filing for bankruptcy and the bank discovering that Gibby didn't have an interest in the Grove even though you verified he did. Or, it may have been your need for money. Whatever you did, you pushed her to her breaking point, and she went for her gun."

"That's pure speculation."

"Florida law says you can't collect on an insurance policy if you participate in the homicide on the insured."

I was trying to prod Adam into a confession.

"You have to prove I killed her."

"Since the DA feels this is a possible homicide, the carrier won't pay the benefits until this is settled in court."

The Sheriff was allowing me to continue only because of his love for Alex. He could see Adam was getting very uncomfortable.

"Adam, we have enough circumstantial evidence to go to court on criminal charges. Then, in a separate court, Alex's estate will petition to be the legitimate beneficiary of the $10 million, not you. The policy may even be declared void and the insurer relieved of paying any proceeds. Then, I will inform the Bar of the various criminal charges and court proceedings. You had a fiduciary relationship, and you were self-dealing."

"Alex was alive when I left," he replied.

Then, the Sheriff leaned forward and said, "Adam, you were there?"

"Oh God, you didn't know, did you. You tricked me."

The Sheriff spoke. "I think we have enough to at least tie you to Sam's death. You needed to cover up. Sam must have told you we were coming to see him again. When you met him that night, he threatened he would tell us about the $10 million policy that you owned."

Adam was silent. He made no attempt to move from his chair.

"You probably put Sam up to filing that complaint about the crop insurance to throw us off. You knew Sam had to die in that fire. Adam, you were scared because Sam was going to disclose the existence of the second life insurance policy."

He continued to just sit there, defeated and speechless. The Sheriff had enough information, and I had nothing else to say.

As the Sheriff rose from his chair he said, "Adam, I'm arresting you."

Before he could completely stand up, Adam pulled a gun from under the desk.

The Sheriff said, "Adam, don't do anything foolish now." The gun was pointed at me.

"Arthur, when you showed up and posed some solutions for Alex, I got worried that maybe you could straighten her out and calm her down and she wouldn't have her temper outbursts. I was counting on her temper combined with her high blood pressure to kill her—and the sooner, the better. I went to see her that morning to tell her there was a second policy on her life. I said that I didn't think she would want or could afford it, so I had had the trust buy it with my money and then had the trust transfer it to myself as trustee. She exploded when I told her what I had done. She said all I wanted was to see her dead. When she went for her gun, I grabbed her arm. She had a violent heart attack and died."

The Sheriff looked at Adam. "Adam, that may be manslaughter at most. Put the gun away."

"No, my life is a financial disaster. I needed the insurance proceeds from the second policy. I borrowed so much money that even selling my limited partnership won't help me. I saw Alex's medical reports. I couldn't believe the carrier would actually issue a policy at a reasonable rate. I never told Alex."

Before the Sheriff could react, Adam turned the gun and shot himself in the head. I hate guns.

The Sheriff looked at me and shook his head in disbelief. We would never know if he killed Sam. My feeling was that Sam was going to tell us about the second policy tomorrow morning and told Adam.

CHAPTER EIGHTEEN

Financial Planning

I stayed at a motel down the road that night, and Goldie stayed with some friends in town. I asked to see her the next morning. She invited me to come to the house where she was staying.

By the time I arrived, Goldie had made all the arrangements for Alex's funeral. She planned to open the house at the Grove and invite all of Alex's friends for a sort of "wake" that night. Alex's children wouldn't be there. Gibby was still in the hospital, Dawn was in a rehab center, and Cindy wasn't invited per the Sheriff's request. Goldie had leaned on the Sheriff, and Cindy and Alex's two grandchildren would be at the funeral.

"I need you there to support me if I get weepy," she said. I assured her that I'd be at the funeral with her.

"Arthur, I have some more news for you."

"What?"

"I want to hire you to help me keep the Grove, not sell it."

"What? Who will run it?"

"Gibby and I."

Goldie caught me totally off guard.

"You have to be kidding."

"No, I spent these last few days with Gibby. I raised him. I watched Alex run the Grove for years. She hired a great crew to maintain it. I can oversee it the same way she did."

I said, "Ok, but Gibby..."

She cut me off. "Gibby will need some major surgery to his knees and then rehab. The doctors told him to lose 100 pounds. When the doctors saw his test results, they told him he has to stop drinking or he'll die. Gibby has agreed to move out to the house on one condition. The house has to be air conditioned." Goldie felt Gibby could learn to love the Grove like Alex did.

"Only time will tell."

"Ok, Arthur, you hot-shot financial planner, what do we do next?"

"It will cost you some money. Not for me, but for a good estate tax attorney. The attorney has to petition the court to remove Adam as the executor and trustee of Alex's estate. You are going to be the executor and trustee."

"Are you sure I'm capable of doing this?"

"Yes, the attorney and I will help you."

"What about the IRS?"

"A year ago they would have argued that 'best use' of the land was development, but now it's greenbelt. Builders and developers are dumping land and options on land. Some big developers are shedding employees. Land values are dropping. In addition, we can argue that Alex was a key person and request a key person discount.[23] So between lack of marketability and key person combined with agricultural usage, the value will be significantly less than my original projections."

"How do we pay the IRS?"

"First, we don't. Not yet, anyhow. There are two valuation dates for property: the date of death and six months later. I think we want to wait to look at six-month values. I think the

[23] *See Glossary, 11.*

current values will fall further. In addition, since more than 35% of Alex's adjusted gross estate will consist of the Grove, we can use a code section called 6166 to just pay interest for four years and then the tax over the next ten years.[24] That gives us fourteen years to get the money together. We do have the $5 million in life insurance that can be used in addition to her investment assets. I don't know what will happen with the $10 million policy. That would be an added bonus. Second, if Gibby will agree to actually run the Grove, we can get the IRS to drop the value by almost $1 million through another code section called 2032A.[25] The estate attorney and Jack Holden can work this out with the IRS. In addition, the Grove is very profitable because of a loss carryforward. We can use the accumulated money to pay taxes."

"It's that easy?"

"Yes, with the right professionals, it's that easy. However, if Gibby actually runs the Grove, he gets paid. But Dawn and Cindy come off the payroll, and we let Jack Holden run the day-to-day accounting by CPA standards."

"How do I get money to Cindy and Dawn?"

"I think we keep the structure of the Grove as an S corporation. Each of the three children owns a third. Gibby will be active whereas Dawn and Cindy will be passive shareholders. Excessive corporate profits above salary and expenses will pass to each of them. Also, you can make distributions from the other trusts based on their needs.

Goldie, you are going to control this?"

"I want to. I raised them."

"How does Gibby feel about me?"

"I wouldn't come around if I were you. Maybe he'll change his mind. I have tried to show him that some good has come out of the shooting."

[24] *See Glossary, 18.*
[25] *See Glossary, 23.*

"As soon as we get the tax attorney involved, I'm moving on," I said quietly. Goldie just nodded in agreement. Now that I had decided on a plan, her self-confidence had returned.

"By the way, Arthur, I can't let you have the trains. I'm keeping them to remind Gibby of what he almost did, and I'm putting them up at Christmas for the grandkids."

Actually, I thought that Alex would like this solution. I was pleased with the outcome. However, the national press and TV had no real news when this all happened. There I was, splashed all over the national news and then the talk shows. Most of it wasn't nice.

One pulp weekly front page read "Financial planner causes three deaths." Fortunately, my practice didn't suffer. Most of my clients thought it was humorous. I didn't. Then there was the call from Harry.

"Hey, Arthur, I've got another murder case for you."

"Yeah, funny."

"Let's see, in the early 1990s I think you had eleven carrier failures due to junk bonds and real estate problems. Is that right?"

Harry and all my friends like to rub this in. At one time I wrote with over one-hundred carriers. I wrote everything from life insurance to property insurance. I had a bad time in 1991 for a variety of reasons. Harry loved to razz me about it.

"Yeah, so what. That's old news."

"So now in four days you get involved in three deaths. That's a new record."

I hung up with Harry. I sat in my chair pondering the case. Goldie, with her enthusiasm and determination, just might be able to pull this family back together. I'd do whatever I could to help her.

And I think Harry owes me a rare antique electric train.

Glossary

1. **Applicable credit amount**: a credit to which the estate of every individual is entitled, which can be directly applied against the gift or estate tax due.

2. **Bargain sale**: part gift, part sale of an asset for some amount that the parties know is less than what would be regarded as full and adequate consideration. The difference between the consideration received by the seller-donor and the value of the asset transferred constitutes a gift for tax purposes.

3. **Beneficiary**: a person who is receiving or will receive a gift of a beneficial interest in property.

4. **Broker**: an individual who arranges and services insurance policies on behalf of the insurance buyer. He or she is the representative of the insured; whereas, an insurance agent is first and foremost the representative of the insurance company.

5. **Bypass trust**: a testamentary trust designed to keep property transferred to it by the decedent spouse out of the surviving spouse's gross estate.

6. **Corporations**:

   a. A **C corporation** is a corporation taxed under Subchapter C of the IRC. Under Subchapter C, income or losses are determined and income taxes are assessed at the entity level. That means that at the end of the year, the C corporation will file a tax return and pay taxes on the money the company has earned. When the shareholders receive distributions or payment from the corporation (not wages), they will pay income tax on the money they receive. In essence, this has been called "double-dipping" or taxed twice. A C corporation files IRS Form 1120 annually.

   b. As an **S corporation**, the business is not taxed as a separate taxable entity. Instead, the entire S corporation's income or losses "pass through" to the shareholders on a pro-rata basis. This means the shareholders report the income (or loss) on their own income tax returns. Although an S corporation must file its own income tax returns, if handled correctly, generally no income taxes are assessed against the corporation. This strategy keeps the owner of the corporation from being taxed twice; first on the money the corporation has earned, then again on the money when he/she pays himself or herself. An S corporation files IRS Form 1120S annually.

There are numerous other advantages and disadvantages to either corporation type.

7. **Crummey provisions**: a general power clause found in some trusts that gives one or more beneficiaries the right to withdraw, for a limited period of time each year, the lesser of the amount of the annual gift exclusion or the value of the gift property transferred into the trust. This allows the donor to claim an annual exclusion for a gift to an irrevocable trust.

8. **Generation-skipping transfer tax (GSST)**: an extra federal tax on certain property to a skip person, that is, someone who is two generations or more younger than the donor.

9. **Gifting** (for gift tax purposes): Property or property rights or interests gratuitously passed or transferred for less than an adequate and full worth to another, in trust or otherwise, directly or indirectly.

10. **Irrevocable life insurance trust**: a trust arrangement in which the trust owns a life insurance policy on an insured's life within the trust.

11. **Key person discount**: a valuation discount may be allowed for a business that loses a key person who was largely responsible for the operation of the business.

12. **1981 Tax Act**: since enactment, virtually all transfers to a spouse, whether made during lifetime or at death, have been tax free; the amount of the transfer is treated as a "marital" deduction from the total gross estate or gross gifts.

13. **Net operating loss (NOL):** a regular corporation deducts an NOL the same way sole proprietors do; the same carryback (two years) and carryforward (20 years). NOLs are more valuable in high-income years when a corporation's top tax rate is high. Thus a carryback NOL can be a good choice for corporations with high-income carryback years. It is not allowed in S corporations.

14. **Policy ownership:** the policy may be owned by the individual on whose life the policy is written, or by the beneficiary, or by someone else.

15. **Qualified subchapter S trust (QSST):** a major issue associated with estate planning for an S corporation business owner and possible business continuation is the restriction on who maybe a succeeding shareholder or owner. Generally, "non-natural persons" (trusts) are not permitted as eligible shareholders. However, a QSST is an exception. Therefore, the QSST can be an owner. Any income or loss passes directly to the income beneficiary.

16. **Revocable trust:** a trust that can be revoked, amended, or terminated by the grantor and the property recovered by the grantor.

17. **Section 179:** an expense deduction is provided for taxpayers who elect to treat the cost of qualifying property as an expense rather than a capital expenditure.

18. **Section 6166** is applicable to estates that create a liquidity crisis due to the death of a business owner. If the estate is eligible, the estate tax for a closely held business interest can be paid over 14 years. The first four annual installments are interest-only payments starting on the one-year anniversary of the original due date.

19. **Spendthrift provision:** trust provisions restricting beneficiaries from assigning trust income or principal interests prior to distribution.

20. **Spousal gift**: under the unlimited marital deduction, gifts to a U.S. citizen spouse are fully deductible, provided that they are not terminable interests.

21. **Testamentary trust**: a trust established by a will. The funding mechanism is the probate process.

22. **Transfer-for-value-rule**: as a general rule, death proceeds from life insurance contracts are exempt from income tax. A basic exception to this rule is any interest in the policy that has been transferred by assignment or otherwise in exchange for valuable consideration. The proceeds will be subject to income tax to the extent that they exceed the consideration paid (and premiums subsequently paid) by the person to whom the policy was transferred.

23. **2032A** (special use valuation): permits qualifying estates to value at least a portion of the real property in the estate at its "qualified use" value, e.g., at its value as a grove, rather than at its highest and best use value. If the election is made, the maximum amount by which the value of special use real estate can be reduced is $750,000 (indexed for inflation).

24. **Universal life policy:** the essential feature which distinguishes it from traditional whole life is that, subject to specified limitations, the premiums, cash value, and level of protection can be adjusted up or down during the term of the contract to meet the owner's needs. Another feature is the fact that the interest credited to the policy's cash value is geared to current interest rates, but is subject to a minimum, such as three percent.

In effect, the premiums under the universal life policy are credited to a fund, and this fund is credited with the policy's share of investment earnings after the deduction of expenses. The fund provides the source of funds to pay for the cost of pure protection under the policy.